D0092988

WORST-CASE CASE COLLIN

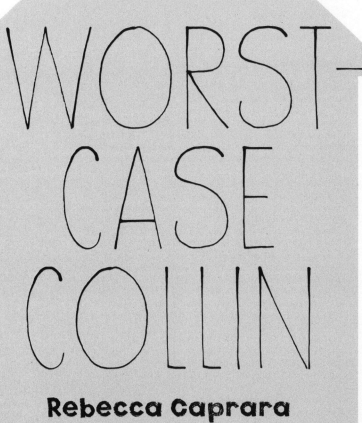

WORST-CASE COLLIN

Rebecca Caprara

ini Charlesbridge

Published by Charlesbridge
9 Galen Street
Watertown, MA 02472
(617) 926-0329
www.charlesbridge.com

Library of Congress Cataloging-in-Publication Data
Names: Caprara, Rebecca, author.
Title: Worst-case Collin / by Rebecca Caprara.
Description: Watertown, MA: Charlesbridge, 2021. | Summary: "In the two
   years since his mother was killed in an automobile crash, Collin has been
   anticipating further disasters, writing down what to do in the event of
   an avalanche or mentally practicing the Heimlich maneuver just in
   case—but the real trouble is that his mathematician father is obsessed
   with a classic math problem and has a hoarding problem that is
   spiraling out of control, leaving Collin desperate to hide this chaos
   from his friends and everyone else, even as he struggles with his own
   grief."—Provided by publisher.
Identifiers: LCCN 2019046483 (print) | LCCN 2019046484 (ebook) |
   ISBN 9781623541453 (hardcover) | ISBN 9781632899224 (ebook)
Subjects: LCSH: Compulsive hoarding—Juvenile fiction. | Bereavement in
   children—Juvenile fiction. | Fathers and sons—Juvenile fiction. |
   Parents—Death—Juvenile fiction. | Mathematicians—Juvenile fiction. |
   Friendship—Juvenile fiction. | CYAC: Novels in verse. | Compulsive
   hoarding—Fiction. | Grief—Fiction. | Death—Fiction. | Fathers and
   sons—Fiction. | Mathematicians—Fiction. | Friendship—Fiction. |
   LCGFT: Psychological fiction.
Classification: LCC PZ7.5.C38 Wo 2021 (print) | LCC PZ7.5.C38 (ebook) |
   DDC 813.6 [Fic]—dc23
LC record available at https://lccn.loc.gov/2019046483
LC ebook record available at https://lccn.loc.gov/2019046484

Printed in the United States of America
(hc) 10 9 8 7 6 5 4 3 2 1

Display type set in Wayang by David Kerkhoff
Text type set in Sabon by Jan Tschichold
Printed by Berryville Graphics in Berryville, Virginia, USA
Production supervision by Jennifer Most Delaney
Designed by Kristen Nobles

For Stefano

BEFORE

I used to dream
about normal stuff like
     making the swim team,
     acing my social studies quiz,
     getting revenge on Liam for pranking me all the time.

These days
my main goal
is to prevent disaster
from striking again.

Or, at the very least,
to be better prepared.

Which is harder
than it sounds
when you're in middle school
     and calamities of various sorts
     occur daily.

AFTER

Now I carry
a bright orange book
in my pocket
at all times.

It has instructions for:
      outrunning killer bees,
      crawling out of quicksand,
      surviving an earthquake.

There's even a part about escaping
from a car submerged in water.

My friend Georgia says,
If any of those things actually happened,
you'd never have the time or wits
to check your little orange book.

She has a good point.
So I'm memorizing every chapter,
starting with the one about the sinking car.

SWIMMING

I've become a good swimmer:
      backstroke,
      freestyle,
      butterfly (which is the most challenging)

My friend Liam is a decent swimmer, too.
But he prefers to invent his own wacky strokes.
Watching him from the pool deck after school
makes me laugh so hard
I snort Gatorade through my nose,
especially when he attempts
the Slippery Noodle Double Kick.

My favorite is sidestroke
because it's low intensity
and can be sustained over long distances
      (handy if you become lost at sea, for example).

Coach Baker says sidestroke,
      along with all of Liam's inventions,
aren't official strokes,
at least not in competition.

That's fine by me.
I'm not in this for speed.
Survival is more important
than winning medals.

SIDESTROKE

Pick a cherry,
put it in your basket.
        One.

Pick a cherry,
put it in your basket.
        Two.

That's what I repeat
in my head
when I practice.

Making sure to avoid
the danger zone
under the diving board.

Pick a cherry,
put it in your basket.
        Three.

I stretch my arms,
kick my legs.
Counting each cherry,
not how many laps I do.
        Which is a lot.

I've been swimming
every day
since the accident.

Except for the days
when lightning threatens

to shock the water
and everyone in it.

Or the days
when the water gets shocked
with chemicals
because some knucklehead
pooped in the pool.

Pick a cherry,
put it in your basket.
          Four.

I swim, swim, swim.
Pick, pick, pick.

The cherries never
weigh me
down.

They're not real,
thankfully.

T-MINUS 119 DAYS

X
    X
       X

Liam makes a calendar—
a countdown
until the last day of school.

Each red X makes him and Georgia giddy
for the freedom of
summer vacation.

Each red X twists my stomach
into a knot.

MATH

The kind of math
my dad teaches
is brain-numbingly hard.

Not like 1 cherry + 1 cherry = 2 cherries.

Dad's math has more letters
than numbers,
which makes
zer0
sense to me.

Then again
I'm not the genius—
      he is.

DAD'S DREAM

For as long as I can remember
my father has dreamed
of solving something
called the Riemann hypothesis.

Lots of very smart people consider this
impossible.

Which only makes Dad
more determined
to figure it out.

Which I think
is very cool.

MAGNIFICENT BOY

Every time we'd visit Dad at work,
the big green quad
buzzed with people
      studying,
      tossing Frisbees,
      lying in the sun like lizards.

Mom would pack a picnic lunch.
Dad would meet us in the shade
on a checkered blanket.

Students would wander over
all starry-eyed.
Hi, Professor Brey, they'd say,
tripping over their words.

Dad would put down his sandwich,
wipe crumbs from his beard,
introduce us:
This is Melody,
my brilliant wife.
And this fine young man is Collin,
my magnificent boy.

Mom would blush,
but I would sit up straight,
suddenly growing
three
inches
taller

basking in his attention
like the sunbathers
soaking up golden rays.

GEORGIA'S DREAM

Georgia says she has the same dream
over and over:
>She goes to school and realizes
>she forgot to get dressed.
>She's so mortified she runs home.

Why do you run home? I ask.

Because I'm buck naked!
Wouldn't you?

To Georgia, home is a safe place.

My turn! My turn! Liam says.
Sometimes I dream
that I go to school.

And?

That's it.

That's it?

Yeah. School's the worst.
Except recess. Recess is the best.

We stare at him.

What? I thought we were sharing nightmares.

I don't share mine.

Worst-Case Scenario #11:
AVALANCHE

- When traveling in areas prone to avalanche, wear a small radio beacon to transmit your location to rescue crews.

- If you feel snow and ice shifting underfoot, attempt to move uphill, above the crack line.

- If you are swept into the avalanche, try to "swim," or thrash, to the top of the snow.

- Reach for the sky, keeping one arm above your head.

- This will help rescuers find you and make climbing out of the snowpack easier.

- If you are buried deep, spit into the snow to create a vital pocket of air.

- Note where gravity carries your saliva. Dig in the opposite direction.

- BREATHE!

NICKNAMES

Tyson and Keith
think they're so hilarious,
making other kids laugh
when they call me names:
       Leggy Peggy
       Sweaty Betty
       Nervous Nelly

Forget grizzly bear attacks and typhoons—
       apparently growth spurts,
       overzealous sweat glands,
       and responsible emergency preparedness
       are the real threats.

DISCOVERY

There were times Before
when an avalanche of ideas
would bury my dad,

when he needed to dig through
mountains of notes and numbers,
clawing and tunneling his way out.

I'd sneak down the stairs,
into the basement,
clutching the railing,

stealing glimpses
of whiteboards
webbed with equations,

stacks of books
rising from the floor
like stalagmites in a cave,

computer screens
washing the room
in a pulsing blue glow.

Dad paced, muttered,
surely on the brink
of a breakthrough.

Discovery is a messy process, Mom would say.
Your father works best
in a state of creative chaos.

COLLECTIONS

Part of that chaos
came from Dad's collections:
> newspaper clippings,
> calculations on napkins,
> pages torn from notebooks.

He was supposed to keep all that stuff
at the university or
in the basement.

If his papers appeared upstairs,
Mom shuffled them into neat stacks
and clipped the important-looking sheets
into fat binders onto labeled shelves.

Then came the broom,
the dustpan,
the garbage bin.

Dad would grimace,
> twitch,
flinch.

Sometimes he'd go out
for a walk,
or take me to Miguel's,
where half a dozen tacos
with extra hot sauce
helped him forget

that Mom was
messing
with his mess.

NUMBERS

Miguel, have I ever asked about your number? Dad said
one afternoon when we visited the taquería together.

Phone number? Miguel asked, loading up a tray with food.
It's right on the sign.

No, a different kind of number.

A lucky number?

I suppose you could call it that.
Everyone has at least one number
they feel connected to.

Ah, yes, I understand.
Miguel winked at me.
He tapped some buttons on the cash register.
Today, Professor Brey,
that number is $11.97!

I knew that made Dad happy,
because both eleven and ninety-seven
are prime numbers—
        his favorite.

8

Mom always chose
the number eight.
She liked its symmetry.

Best of all
8
is an upright

            infinity

      looping   looping

          looping

     around   around

        around.

No beginning
or end
because she was
supposed to be
with us
forever.

PRIME TIME

In class Ms. Treehorn says,
*Can anyone tell me
what a prime number is?*

Me! Me! Sabrina, the class kiss-up, squeals.

Georgia's hand rockets up, too.
Collin can!

I shoot eyeball laser beams at her.
But Georgia keeps smiling,
like she's doing me a favor.

Go ahead, Collin.

Sabrina huffs.
Everyone stares at me.
I have no choice.

*A prime number
can only be divided evenly
by one and itself.*

*Wonderful!
Thank you, Collin.
Now can anyone tell—*

Collin's dad is a mathematician, Georgia interrupts,
still wearing that smile.
*He's solving one of the most important
math problems in the world.*

What kind of dork squad decides that? Keith snickers.

The Clay Mathematics Institute, I mumble.

Boring! Tyson groans,
which sounds like *BOH-RANG!*

*He'll get a million dollars
if he gets it right,* Georgia says.

That grabs everyone's attention,
especially Ms. Treehorn,
who's skilled at sniffing out
dreaded little things called
          learning moments.

Collin, is this true?

I nod the blazing tomato
that is my head.

*How fascinating.
Tell us more!*

If you want to make
scrambled eggs
out of my brain,
ask me about
the Riemann hypothesis.

If you want to see
my father light up
like a Christmas tree,
ask him about it.

I wish Ms. Treehorn
would just forget
about this stupid
learning moment.

She won't.

So I recite something Dad's said a billion times:
It's a conjecture that the Riemann zeta function
has its zeros only at the negative even integers and . . .

The room is silent.
Even Ms. Treehorn blinks,
head cocked, confused.

Yeah, I don't really get it either, I say.
My palms sweat.
It has something to do with prime numbers.
It's one of the Millennium Prize Problems.

And your father is really working on a proof?

He's . . . trying.
But the truth is
I'm not so sure anymore.

2

2 is a prime number.

2 is the number of years
that have passed since Before became After.

2 is the number of cars
that collided on the bridge.

2 is the number of states
separated by the river that runs under the bridge.

2 is the number of minutes
it took emergency responders to break the window.

2 is too many.

2 is the number of people
left in our home now that Mom is gone.

2 is not enough.

MOVING FORWARD

The weeks
         and months
    after the accident
were a
    blur.

Dad didn't go back
to work right away.
The university said
he should take some time.

I wanted to stay home with him,
but Aunt Lydia
and Liam's mom, Sharon,
and even a grief therapist
said school and routine
would help me
        move forward.

        Except
        I just wanted to go
backward.

REMEMBERING

I never stood a chance
against Mom's morning
smooch attacks.

Go away, I mumbled
even though I knew
she never left for work
without saying goodbye.

Mom poked me in the ribs
once, twice, three times.

I squirmed, sat up,
rubbed crusties from my eyes,
and surrendered.

Thatta boy.
She hugged me hard.
I hugged her back but
                                    I pulled away
before she could plant
some horribly embarrassing
pink pucker mark
on my cheek.

That lipstick Mom wore
must've been a mix of
permanent marker and superglue.
No matter how hard I rubbed,
her kisses refused to budge.

Right as she was about to launch
another attack,
her watch beeped.

Ha! I dove out of reach.

Saved by the bell, she said,
her laughter bright
as the dawn sun
peeking over the horizon.

She stood, yawned,
straightened her scrubs,
and placed a slip of paper
on the bedside table.

A BETTER GOODBYE

Mom left me checklists
whenever she worked
early-morning shifts at the hospital.

The lists helped me
worry
less

and helped Dad
focus
more.

This one said:

☐ Get dressed
☐ Wash face
☐ Do the funky chicken dance
☐ Eat breakfast
☐ Brush teeth
☐ Battle fire-breathing dragon
☐ Pack homework
☐ Go to school

She always added a few silly things,
claiming I needed to
lighten up a little,
      be less of a
      worrywart.

∞ ∞ ∞

Wait! I said. *What about my lunch?*

Oh, shoot! I'm sorry, Collin.
She glanced at her watch.
I don't have time right now.

Mooooom!

It's fine, bud. Dad will take care of it.

I groaned. The last time
Dad had packed my lunch,
he'd given me a Tupperware
full of bean salad. Seriously.

If you thought a smooch attack was bad,
try surviving
a bean-induced gas attack
during a post-lunch game of dodgeball.

Mom patted my shoulder.
I'll make it up to you. Promise.

Before she closed the door
Mom said,
        I love you.

I should've said,
        Have a good day
or
        Drive safe
or
        I love you, too.

But I was still
tired and grumpy
so instead
I only muttered
two words:
      Bean. Salad.

I wish so badly
I could have said

      a better goodbye.

GOING BACK

When Dad eventually returned to work
after the accident
he discovered
that someone had been using his office.

He was convinced
this new colleague was
       stealing precious equations,
       unlocking the secrets
       of his almost-solved
       million-dollar math.

Dad complained
to the dean,
who explained
there was a shortage
of space on campus.

She assured my father
that many faculty members
enjoyed shared offices.

When Dad put up a fight,
he was told to
embrace collaboration
       or find a new place to work.

That's when he started
bringing all his files home.

LAYERS

Without someone to keep
Dad's collections in check,
layers accumulate
like the sedimentary rock formations
Ms. Treehorn taught us about.

It happens so slowly at first
I don't really notice, until
       papers
              cardboard
       magazines
replace
       carpet
            tile
       hardwood.

I try to tidy up, throw things   away.

But Dad gets all twitchy, so I let it   go.

GROSSBOMBS

Liam slides a plastic baggie
across the lunch table.

Jawbreakers! Georgia squeals.
Dibs on the purple one!
She plucks a candy from the bag.

These are most definitely choking hazards,
so I start explaining each step
of the Heimlich maneuver to my friends
before choosing a red candy,
hoping it's cinnamon-flavored.

Georgia's nose scrunches,
mashing her freckles together.
She drops the candy into her palm,
inspects it—first purple, now acid green.
She shrugs, pops it back into her mouth.

I roll mine across my tongue,
cautiously passing it from cheek to cheek.
It tastes like cherry, then grape, then . . .

I realize too late
that Liam's smile
is a smirk.

Sour bitterness—
one hundred million times infinity worse
than anything the lunch ladies have ever served—
affronts my taste buds.

Georgia and I double over, gagging.
Liam doubles over, laughing.

We recover, sit up, and fire
spit-covered ammunition
from the cannons of our mouths
straight at Liam.

Prank candy, suckers! he cheers,
savoring the sweet taste of our suffering.
They're called GrossBombs.
Found 'em at the Henny Penny.
Pretty awesome, huh?

More like awesomely revolting.
Georgia wags her tongue
like a dog panting on a hot day.

I chug chocolate milk,
trying to wash away the taste.

Liam pulls a box from his backpack,
reads the label:
A deceptively delicious outer coating
hides a truly gross explosion of flavor!

Ick! Prepare for payback, you punk, Georgia warns.

She might talk tough,
but Georgia has
a forgiving heart.

THE STATE OF MY HEART

```
         mom              mom
     missing mom      missing mom
 missing mom missing mom missing mom
 missing mom missing mom missing mom
 missing mom missing mom missing mom
    mom missing mom missing mom
     missing mom missing mom
         missing mom
             mom
              !
```

BULLIES

Watch it, Leggy Peggy!
I hear Tyson's voice,
but I don't see
his sneaker

                       stuck out
in the aisle.

The linoleum floor has little green flecks
I've never noticed before.

Tyson and Keith
explode with laughter
as sour-bitter-nasty
as that prank candy.

You okay? Georgia kneels by my side.

Aww. He needs his girlfriend to help him up.

I am not his girlfriend, Georgia snaps.
Then, to me, she mutters,
Sorry, Collin, that didn't come out right.
Just ignore them.

I nod, trying to also ignore
the hives rising up my neck,
the sweat soaking through my shirt.

I tug too-short jeans, trying to cover
clumsy, too-long legs,
wondering when
this body, this life,
will feel like my own again.

Worst-Case Scenario #432:
RIPTIDE

- If you are caught in a riptide, do not struggle against the current.

- Swim parallel to shore.

- Reserve your energy by floating on your back.

- Once the riptide subsides, attempt to swim back to shore.

- STAY CALM!

OUTSIDE

My house is yellow.
The trim is blue.
The stucco is chipped a little here
                              and there.

The window boxes have been empty for a while,
but Dad pays a landscape guy twenty bucks
to spruce up the yard every few months.

He says when I turn fourteen,
he'll let me mow the lawn.
As if I'd jump at the chance
to operate a machine
with sharp, spinning blades.

It doesn't matter, though.
Grass barely grows in Bullhead's heat.
Plus, our mower is buried
somewhere in the garage,
where a litter of raccoons
or maybe armadillos
is probably curled up on the engine,
cozy beneath the rubble
of newspapers, random yard signs,
and a thousand pink plastic flamingos
that Dad bought on special
when the garden center went out of business.

The point is, our house looks
borderline normal
from the   outside.

But
opening the door
is like licking the cherry coating off
a GrossBomb.
You don't want to do it.

SPECTACULAR DEAL

I can't do my homework
at the kitchen table
because today it's covered
with clothes.

I hope there's a pair of longer pants
or looser shorts for me, but
it's all women's clothing.

My heart does a loop-de-loop.
Maybe Dad has been cleaning out the closets.
Maybe he is finally letting go.

Then I see tags, tags, tags.
I sift through the pile.
My hand brushes something lacy.
I jump back.
          Gross.
Ladies' underwear does not belong
on the kitchen table.

At least it's new, with tags.

Dad emerges,
headphones blasting one of his favorite
Yann Tiersen piano compositions.

Dad! I shout.
Dad! I wave a bright pink something in his direction like a flag.
I really hope it's not another pair of underpants.

He looks up, unplugs.
Hey, bud.

What's all this? I ask.

Big sale at the Rummage Room today.

Wait. That means somebody wore all this stuff before . . .
I have a sudden urge to wash my hands.

Everything's in excellent condition.
He picks up a bra
with the most gigantic boob cups I've ever seen.
If I had a conjoined twin, we could wear
that monstrosity on our heads like a double hat.

I can't decide
if I should laugh
or barf.

Wednesday is half-price day.
And I had a bonus coupon!
A spectacular deal,
too good to pass up.

But, Dad, this is girl stuff.
Who's going to wear it?

He surveys the heap.
His fingers
fidget,
          tremble . . .

He mumbles,
his voice
small,
      brittle.

Before I can remind him
      that Mom's never coming back,
the headphones clamp over his head,
cords like tentacles
pulling him farther

and farther

away.

LOST

Dad? Dad?

I
  follow
      him
          down
              the
                  basement
                          stairs . . .

                          I only make it
                          halfway
                          before I stop—
                                  shocked
                          to see
                                          piles,
once mesmerizing,
              now
              in total   disarray.
                                  So eerie.
          Just plain   creepy,
                                              glowing
                  in the bluish
                  light.
                      Growing
                              bigger,
                                  faster,

                                  than ever before.

T-MINUS 108

We have a swim meet
in two weeks.
Coach Baker says
a scout will be there.

Georgia stays at the pool
later
and later,
practicing her dives.

I stay, too,
to practice a little.
But mostly to
    hang out with Georgia,
    avoid Tyson and Keith,
    and postpone going home.

HIGH DIVE

Georgia's wet toes
cling to the
        edge
of the diving
platform.

She's calm,
happy even,
teetering on the
        brink.

I wish I felt
the same
but I hate
c
l
i
m
b
i
n
g
up
there.

My vision goes
wobbly; my brain
floods
with worries.

I'd much rather swim laps,
nice and flat, back and forth.

Georgia inhales.

Her knees
become springs.
Her body,
a brave spear.
Straight fingertips,
pressed palms,
the arrowhead.

She's much more graceful now
than the day we met.

WARM WELCOME

A little over two years ago
our fourth-grade teacher announced
that a new girl would be joining our class.

I remember Liam whispering,
Whoopee-cushion welcome?
Itching-powder handshake?
I could probably find some spiders
to put in her desk!

I shook my head firmly. *No.*

I had transferred to Bullhead City Elementary a year earlier
so I knew
       it was hard enough to be the new kid
       without a bunch of doofus pranksters
       putting spiders in your desk.

Aw, come on, Liam whined.
Pranks are harmless. They're fun!
You do remember what fun is, right?

Sure, I do.
But your pranks are too . . .
I searched for the right word.
Unpredictable.

Dude, duh. That's the point.

Just leave the new girl alone. Okay?

GEORGIA

Turned out, the joke was on us.
Or, rather, on me. Literally.

The first time I met Georgia
she nearly killed me.

One minute
I was splashing around in the pool
hollering *Polo!*
to Liam's *Marco!*

The next minute
out of nowhere
this girl plummeted out of the sky—
                    a human cannonball

                              landing
                               smack
                                dab

                                 on
                                 my
                                head.

UNEXPECTED

The lifeguard helped me out of the water.
He gave me a thorough checkup,
called me a *resilient little dude.*

*I'm never swimming
under the diving board again,* I told Mom later.

That's probably a good idea, she agreed.

And I'm staying far away from that new girl!

*Really? The lifeguard said she stuck around
to make sure you were okay.*

She did, I replied grudgingly.

And she shared her root beer with you, right?

I nodded. She actually let me have the whole can.
She was either very generous or didn't want to swap germs.

*Still, I could have gotten
a bloody nose,
a concussion,
a broken neck!*

But you didn't, Mom reminded me gently,
tempering my fears
with happier possibilities.
*Look on the bright side:
you dodged disaster
AND made a new friend in the process.*

New friend? I scoffed. *I'm not so sure . . .*

But Mom had a knack
for seeing things
other people missed.

BLOOM

We used to plant flowers
in window boxes
at the front of our house.

Every spring
Mom and I visited the garden center
that smelled like fresh, wet dirt.

We'd start with an empty black tray
and leave with a rainbow:
        orange marigolds,
        red geraniums,
        purple ones with smiley-looking faces.

Mom always bought a few
without flowers,
just leaves and
hard green buds.

Why not get the prettier ones? I asked.

These have potential.
They'll surprise us
and give us beauty
when all the others
have stopped
blooming.

FULL

Back then,
our house felt

        full.

Bursting, even.
But never

        crowded,
        cluttered,
        claustrophobic.

Because

        love

doesn't take up
too much room.

GROWTH

Now
the basement
fills up. Books and
binders jam and crowd
already-packed bookshelves.
Couch cushions hide reams of paper.
More magazines and newspapers than any
human could read in an entire lifetime collect in
piles, heaps, mountains, joined by clothing, both clean
and not so clean, that no longer fits in dressers or closets.
Then come bins and boxes of items that have nothing
to do with mathematics, like scarves and gloves and
coupons and cheese graters and broken keyboards.
Spills, drips, leaks seep down through each layer,
inviting mold and rot to flourish. Dust settles like
snowfall, and each day there is less and less and less and
less space for me. I learn to tiptoe around the house.
There may be something dangerous hiding below the surface.

BAFFLED

I'm baffled, pondering
whether Dad's brilliant brain
understands something special
about these random
    scraps
           thingamajigs
      knickknacks
               bric-a-brac
         hunks of junk
that my lesser brain
does not.

The way
Mom knew
to buy the plants
with the hard green buds.

Otherwise,
why would he hang on
to all this stuff?

HISTORY

We're starting a new unit
on Arizona.

Ms. Treehorn says,
Patayan, Mojave, Chemehuevi
and many others were here
long before us.
Long before
anyone called this place Bullhead.

We will learn about
language, culture, history, and more.

She says,
It's important
to understand
where we come from.
To respect
those who came before,
and those we live alongside now.
To appreciate
the places
that make us
who we are.

I can't help but think about
the mess at home.

What does it mean
if you come from garbage?

T-MINUS 101

On Friday
Liam's mom, Sharon,
pulls me inside
their bright, loud, clean home.

Her thin arms are as strong
as two boa constrictors.
Liam says she's been doing yoga.

Sheer madness here! As usual, she says.
Unlike my house, this chaos—
      dogs barking, television blaring, dishes clanking—
is of the cheerful variety.

Coming here for a sleepover
feels like a mini-vacation.

Sharon gives me one more
bone-crushing hug.
So? How are you, babe?

It should be weird
that Liam's mom
calls me babe.

But she's been calling me that
since I first stepped into this house,
nearly three and a half years ago.

Plus, she's feeding me dinner tonight
      (and she makes really good lasagna)
so I let the nickname slide.

THE BLOB

Liam rented *The Blob*
for our sleepover.
He promises
it'll be funny,
not scary.

Don't worry.
Special effects were totally weak
back in the olden days.

Sharon yells from the kitchen,
Hey! 1958 is not
the olden days!

But she must agree
about the not-so-scary part,
otherwise I don't think she'd let us watch it.

Liam grabs the DVD case.
He reads the description,
his voice dropping
low and deep
Indescribable . . .
Indestructible . . .
Nothing can stop it!
THE BLOB!

When the movie starts,
I watch in horror
as the Blob consumes
everything,
everyone
in its path.

Growing bigger and bigger
                    and BIGGER.

Eventually the air force uses a cargo plane
to transport the Blob to the Arctic,
parachuting it onto ice.

Is it finally gone? For good? I ask the television.

A character named Dave says,
The Blob is not dead!
But at least it has been stopped!

The movie ends with a guy named Steve saying,
As long as the Arctic stays cold . . .

Liam's sister, Lindsay, flips on the lights.
I jump.
I look over at Liam.

Uh-oh. He's wide-eyed.

What? What! I shout.

I've got two words for you: Global. Warming.

I gasp.
Liam laughs.
Lindsay laughs, too.

It's only a movie, Collin.
Don't freak out.
It isn't real.

GENIUS

That night
I dream about
the Blob.

It starts in the basement,
devours the staircase,
filling rooms,
blocking doors,
until there's nowhere
for me to go.

I climb
to the roof.
      Cling
to the chimney.
           Cry
              for help.

Dude! Doooooood!
Someone shakes me
awake.

My chest heaves
up and
      down.
My pajamas are clammy
with sweat.

Dude! Liam repeats.
You're a flipping genius!

Huh?
I sit up and look around the dark room.

You were talking in your sleep.

What did I say?

Just the most brilliant thing ever.

Really? I try to catch my breath.

You kept muttering,
To the roof! To the roof!

Oh! Wait. Why is that genius?

Duh! Jell-O.

I scratch my head and fall
back asleep.

∞ ∞ ∞

In the morning,
we tie safety tethers
made from bedsheets
to our waists,
lean out
Liam's bedroom window
          (because there is no way we're actually climbing up
          to the roof)
and drop Jell-O
onto the ground below,
pretending the wobbly snack
is the Blob,
just like in the movie.

We make tiny parachutes
out of paper napkins.
Let 'em fly!
Splat!
Adios, you nasty jiggly monster!

This is fun, I say, releasing a quivery green cup.

Hey, it was your idea!

Right. Because I'm a flipping genius! I laugh.

Maybe Dad and I
have something in common after all.

IMPOSSIBLE

When Dad picks me up,
I ask if we can play
a game of mini-golf
at the new course in town.

*Just a warning—the kids at school
said the obstacles are totally impossible,* I tell him.

Dad's face lights up,
like I hoped it would.

Impossible, huh?
He musses my shaggy brown hair.
We'll see about that . . .

HOLE IN ONE

Before we get started,
I assess all potential mini-golf hazards.
We apply sunblock (UV exposure),
purchase extra-large fountain sodas (hydration),
double-knot our shoelaces (trip prevention).

The course has whirling windmills,
sharp-toothed sharks,
even a sinking pirate ship.
But these are just-for-fun props,
most likely harmless.

Dad likes to analyze
the precise angle and velocity and who-knows-what
of each putt.
I don't have the patience for all that,
yet somehow on the fourth hole
        I sink a hole in one!

Dad erupts,
whooping and cheering so loudly
we almost get kicked out.

By the end of the day
my cheeks are sore
from smiling.

Missing Mom takes up
so much heartspace,
I almost forgot
how much I missed
this version of Dad,
        this version of us.

Worst-Case Scenario #441:
ROCK CLIMBING

- When rock climbing, inspect all harnesses, ropes, helmets, carabiners, etc., before beginning.

- Choose your climbing route wisely and manage risks as you go.

- If you are climbing with a partner, decide who will lead and who will belay.

- Communicate with your climbing partner frequently as you ascend.

- Always keep the rope between you and the wall so you don't become tangled.

- If you think you might fall, look down for obstructions in your path.

- Try for a soft landing with your feet, keeping your hands at the ready.

- If you begin to free-fall, reach for available holds, such as rock ledges or tree branches.

- HANG ON!

SWEATY BETTY

First thing Monday morning,
Tyson elbows me in the hallway.
Outta my way, Sweaty Betty.
Ugh. Ever heard of deodorant?

Can you stop being so rude? Georgia says.

Looks like his girlfriend's sticking up for him again.
I think she needs a nickname, too.
Tyson glares at Georgia.
He nudges his sidekick, Keith.

Uhhhh . . . how about Freckle Face?

Real original. Tyson scowls.
That's the best you got?

She has all those freckles, so . . .

Shut your pieholes! Liam shouts.
If he were a cartoon,
smoke would be pouring
from his ears.

Make us, Loser Face, Keith taunts.

Not worth it. Georgia holds Liam back.

I'm glad my friends
want to protect me,
but Liam gets into enough trouble
on his own
without fighting my battles.

I pull a hoodie from my locker,
tug it on,
try to disappear inside.

Most boys my age
wear wrinkled shirts,
grass-stained jeans,
and smell
a little bit.
I thought I could blend in
until Dad does the laundry again.

But that's not happening anytime soon.

Maybe I can sneak
a few things into the wash at Liam's
the next time I sleep over.

Otherwise, I'll have to
use our washing machine.
But it's in the basement
and that place seriously
creeps me out.

KEEPING BUSY

When I was five years old,
Aunt Lydia had a baby
and Mom flew across the country
from Arizona to Maine
to help for a week.

Before she left, Dad said,
*Melody, what will we do
without you?*

*You'll be fine, Ogden.
Just keep busy.*

Dad took me to work with him,
let me sample all the soft-serve flavors
in the campus dining hall.
At home we played games, built forts,
stayed up late watching television.

When Mom returned,
she found the house
in shambles.

I was still awake
close to midnight
sitting in the living room
on a mountain
of papers, toys, books, blankets, and crayons,
gnawing on a candy bar.

Where is your father? she asked
wiping chocolate from my face,

wrapping me in her arms
like I was Aunt Lydia's new baby,
even though I was much older.

It's way past your bedtime, bud.
She nuzzled my neck,
        then stopped.
Sniffed my hair.
Sniffed my shirt.
Inspected behind my ears.
When was the last time you had a bath?

I counted on my fingers.
One, two, three, four, five, six . . .
seven? Seven!
I smiled
showing all my teeth,
unbrushed for seven days.

∞ ∞ ∞

No baths.
No bedtime.
Candy bars for dinner.
Those had been the perks
of Mom's absence.

Except her face,
suddenly folded with lines,
didn't seem to agree.

I couldn't tell if I was in trouble
or not.

After a bath
with extra bubbles,
toothbrushing
with extra paste,
she dressed me
in fresh pajamas.
Tucked me into bed
with extra kisses
that told me
I wasn't in trouble
at all.

But I couldn't sleep.
The air felt
crackly,
full of static,
ready to spark.

∞ ∞ ∞

She was usually
so patient.
        Except
        that night
Mom was so mad
she yelled at Dad
in a voice
I didn't even know
she had.

The sound
made tiny hairs
stand up
on the back of my neck,

near that spot she'd just scrubbed and scrubbed
until a week's worth of grime
was finally gone.

I cupped my hands
around my ears
in the darkness,
trying to make them bigger, better
sound funnels.

Only a few of the
loudest
broken words
    made it
        up the stairs
            past
              the closed door.

Most were grown-up words
I didn't understand, like
        squalor
            hygiene
    hazardous
      distracted
          nutrition
 reckless
       neglect

∞ ∞ ∞

In the morning
the house was
sparkling clean.

Mom looked up from
scrambling eggs, slicing fruit.
She smiled so big,
I could see all of her
sparkling teeth.

But her eyes were
heavy pebbles.
Her hands, raw.

Sorry we made such a big mess, I said softly,
wanting to make her feel better. Wanting
to make the tightness in my chest
disappear.

Aww, bud. I love you, she said.

I love you a million times infinity to the infinity power.
I jabbed the eggs on my plate.
Can I have a candy bar for breakfast?

She laughed. *Not a chance.*
Zero times infinity to the infinity power.

Even though it would've been nice
to eat another candy bar,
somewhere deep inside
I was thinking,
Maybe you shouldn't go away again.

Her pebble eyes
ringed in red told me
she was thinking
the same.

NICKNAME

Liam decides we seriously need
better nicknames.
He wants to be called Matchstick.

*Because of your red hair or
your fiery temper?* I ask.
He punches my shoulder,
which I think is a yes to both.

I suggest Arrow for Georgia,
since that's what she looks like when she dives.
But Liam says there's a superhero called that.

Georgia likes my idea, though,
so she picks Gannet, a bird that can dive
sixty feet underwater at high speeds.

And mine?

They whisper,
then decide to call me
Worst-Case Collin.

I think this is the worst nickname
EVER.

It was meant as a compliment, Georgia says
when she sees me sulking.
*Because you're always so prepared.
If there were ever some crazy catastrophe,
you're the one I'd want by my side.*

Catastrophe's already taken, Liam says, half listening.

Huh?

My sister's new boyfriend.
At least that's what Mom calls him
behind Lindsay's back. He chuckles.
Anyway, Worst-Case Collin is way better
than Sweaty Betty.

I slug him back.
I hate when he's right.

BRAVERY

On the bus ride home,
I keep thinking about
what Georgia said.

If some crazy thing really does happen one day,
       will I be ready?
       Will I be brave?
       Will I be able to help?

Or will I just be
       a total catastrophe?

Worst-Case Scenario #558:
STARVATION

- If you become lost or stranded without an adequate food supply, insects can provide necessary sustenance for survival.

- They are highly nutritious, rich in fats, proteins, and carbohydrates.

- In some parts of the world, they are even considered a delicacy.

- To collect insects for consumption, search under stones or attract them with a light at night.

- Termites, locusts, crickets, and ant larvae are excellent choices.

- Avoid brightly colored bugs, which may be poisonous.

- Brush or wash away loose dirt.

- Remove hard shells, wings, stingers, and barbed legs.

- For best taste, boil until tender or roast until crunchy and delicious.

- BON APPÉTIT!

HUNTING

My stomach is
growly as a bobcat,
but Dad must be working late,
so I go hunting for dinner alone.

Despite what my book says,
I'm not nearly desperate enough
to eat bugs,
although I could have a feast,
I find so many
in our kitchen.

An entire colony crawls
inside an old takeout container,
feasting on something
that may have, once, resembled
a cheeseburger.

It's hard to tell
if the ache in my gut
is from disgust
or hunger
or missing Mom
        or all of the above.

I throw out the container
and search the cupboard.
A can of corn looks promising.
If only I could find a can opener
or something sharp.
        Of course, I can't.

When you have so much stuff,
it's hard to find anything.

Ms. Treehorn would call it
    counterintuitive,
    a fancy word
    that means
    different
    from what you expect.

I can think of some other vocabulary
to describe the situation here.
    (The sorts of words that land Liam
    in the principal's office on a regular basis.)

I eventually discover
a tin of water chestnuts
with a pull-tab top.

I'm feeling
a lot of things.
    Picky is not
    one of them.

I peel the metal back.
The chestnuts are crunchy,
a little bit salty.
I eat them all.
I even drink the leftover liquid.
There's no sense dumping it
down the drain.
The sink is filled with mail.

The trash can is full
and I can't bear to add
to the mess,
so I take the empty tin
outside and toss it
into the neighbor's blue recycling box
when no one is looking.

MISSING CHAPTER

My orange book
is missing
a chapter.

I read it
cover to cover,
but there are no instructions
for how to survive
what's happening
at home.

For now
the easiest thing to do
is avoid it.

VACANT LOT

There's a huge swath
of emptiness
           on the outskirts
of town.

I ride my bike
all the way there
by myself.

I should tell someone
where I'm going.
      (My worst-case scenario handbook says this is
very important.)
But I never do.
That would defeat
the purpose.

In the distance,
heat smudges the horizon
in thick, wavy strokes,
making it hard to tell where
earth ends
         sky begins.

Up close,
I see thirsty-looking scrub,
clusters of cracked rock,
ideal conditions for:
      stinging scorpions,
      rattling snakes,
      prickling cacti.

Despite these dangers,
        I love it.

In this wide-open
borderless space,
Before and   After
melt
into one
and I feel
closest
        to Mom.

A MEMORY

Even after her shifts at the hospital ended,
Mom still carried her patients in her heart.

I'd do my homework at the kitchen table
while she cooked dinner,
and we'd talk about our days.

She remembered everyone,
even if they were only in her care
for a few hours.

Of course she memorized
important medical stuff like:
       allergies,
       blood pressure,
       history of stroke.

But also stuff like:
       has a cat named Rumpus,
       prefers vanilla pudding,
       likes to watch game shows.

It was hard for anyone
not to love her.

HEALING

The other thing Mom used to tell me
about her patients was this:

> *The ones who laugh*
> *heal faster.*
>
> *I don't understand*
> *the science behind it,*
> *but I see it*
> *all the time.*
>
> *Collin, if there are ever days*
> *when laughing seems too hard,*
> *just start with a smile*
> *and see where it takes you.*

TRYING

I try to follow
Mom's advice,
but some days
are more challenging
than others.
With Tyson and Keith
always teasing me at school,
and the embarrassing, maddening
mess at home,
I'm grateful
for friends
who make me laugh.
Even if Liam is
a complete doofus
most of the time.

T-MINUS 96

On our way to Georgia's house after swim practice,
we stop at the Henny Penny,
      where a massive penny-candy counter stretches from
one end of the store to the other.

As Liam and I fill paper bags with jelly beans,
he sings at the top of his lungs,
Beans, beans! Good for your heart!
The more you eat, the more you—

Mrs. Finnick, the owner of the Henny Penny,
flies down the aisle and hushes Liam
before he gets to the best part of the song.

I worry she'll kick us out of the store
forever. That would be inconvenient.
I worry I might never get to eat another jelly bean
again. That would be tragic.

Georgia puts on a serious face,
apologizes for the disruption.

As soon as Mrs. Finnick turns her back, though,
Georgia's lips lift into a smile
                    warm as the Arizona sunshine
and I don't feel worried
anymore.

HOME STATE

*Today's Arizona-themed topic will be
local entomology,* Ms. Treehorn announces the next morning.

Boh-rang, Tyson moans.

Well, I think it sounds absolutely fascinating! Sabrina says.

I slump down in my chair, frowning.
I learn enough about bugs
from my own kitchen these days.

The projector flickers.
A giant hairy scorpion
flashes onto the wall.

Everyone jolts back in their seats.
Sabrina nearly faints.
A few kids yelp.
I'm pretty sure one of them is Tyson.

If Liam wasn't at the principal's office,
he'd call Tyson out, give him a dose
of his own medicine.
Hey, Wimpy Pants! he'd say.
*You're not scared
of a buggy-wuggy, are you?*

*Did you know fifty-six species of scorpions
call our home state home?* Ms. Treehorn says brightly,
as if this is good news.

I actually do know this.
I also know that

      (thankfully)
only one species
      (the bark scorpion)
has a lethal sting.

This cute little fellow is an Arizonan,
just like all of you!
Ms. Treehorn watches us squirm in our seats.
I think she might be enjoying this.
Not so boring after all, is it?

Out of the corner of my eye,
I see Tyson staring at the scorpion,
shaking his leg, scratching his head,
brushing his shoulders.
Check my back, he whispers to Keith.
I think something's crawling on me.

There's nothing there.

You sure? Tyson hisses.

Uh-huh.

I pretend to listen
to Ms. Treehorn, but mostly
I'm studying that fake-brave bully
getting all twitchy,

the same way Dad acts
when I leave the front door open too long
      or try to clean up his stuff.

APPEARANCES

My father wears a sweater vest
every single day.
Even in the Arizona heat.

He also wears huge
egg-shaped glasses
rimmed in silver
that make him look smart.
Which he is
when it comes to stuff like:
      astrophysics,
      aeronautics,
      advanced calculus.

Oddly,
he's dumb as bricks
about other stuff like:
      laundry,
      dishwashing,
      overbuying.

Which is why
I can never invite my friends over.

So when Georgia says,
*Let's hang out
at your place today, Collin!*

I'm prepared
with excuses.

We're having the walls repainted, I lie.

We won't touch the walls.

Let's build a megafort in the living room, says Liam.
We haven't done that in ages!

Can't. Fumes are too strong.
Chemical inhalation can cause dizziness, nausea, headache . . .

All right, Worst-Case Collin. We get it. He rolls his eyes.
How about the basement?

No one's allowed down there.
It's where my dad keeps his work files.
I don't mention his other
strange collections.

Bummer. What about your room? Liam prods.

It's being painted, too.

Really? What color?

Man, these two are persistent!
My eyes scan the bleachers.
They land on Liam's gym bag.

Ummm, orange.

You're painting your room orange? Georgia says.

What's wrong with orange?
I grab a basketball from Liam's bag.

Nothing, I guess.
It's just a little . . . bright.

Bright is nice, I say, thinking of our curtains
always pulled shut.

I think orange is cool!
Liam snatches the ball from me,
twirls it on his finger,
like a total showboat.

Thank you, Matchstick. I agree.
Let's shoot some hoops.
We can go to my house another day.

Georgia takes the bait
and the ball.
Fine. But we're playing HORSE and I go first.

Suit yourself, Gannet.
Just be prepared to L-O-S-E!
Liam takes off running toward the court.

Hurry up, Worst-Case Collin!
For some reason
when Georgia calls to me—
      grinning like that,
      with her long black ponytail swishing over her shoulder—
my dumb nickname
doesn't sound so bad.

STINKING

I come home
from the basketball court
sweating, stinking, happy,
in desperate need
of a shower.

It would not be unusual
for a kid to have rubber duckies
in his tub.

Rubber tires on the other hand?
Highly unusual.

And yet
that's what I discover.

Five snow tires
to be exact.
Too heavy and awkward
for me to move
by myself.

I guess they will stay,
and I will
go

shower in Dad's bathroom,
if there is any
space.

THE HOARD IS BORN

Late at night
when the rest of the house is quiet,
I swear I hear
      munching,
            crunching,
                  scratching.
I imagine mice, bugs, and
little crawly critters
claiming my home
as their own.

Shhhh. Listen.

Are these noises real?
Or am I just imagining
more worst-case scenarios?
Either way, it's freaking me out.

To distract myself,
I think about nicknames.
I decide to name
the rotten
dust-covered
room-filling
sick-making
pest-attracting
friend-repelling thing
inside my home.

I shall call it
      the Hoard.

REFUGE

Outside,
there are lots of safe places:
>   my friends' houses,
>   the pool,
>   the vacant lot.

Inside,
my bedroom
is the only
refuge.

From now on
I'll keep my door
closed tightly
so the Hoard stays
>   OUT!

BUS

The school bus is not exactly on my list
of safe places.

First of all, the seat belt situation is atrocious.
Most of the straps are frayed,
and the buckles are gunked up with old chewing gum.
No one bothers to use them
        (except me).

Second, the adult-to-kid ratio is absurd.
A single bus driver cannot possibly keep a watchful eye
on fifty-seven students
and still operate a large vehicle in a safe manner.

Third, Tyson rides the same route as me.

At least he sits in the back,
with his older stepbrother, Jax,
and a bunch of goonish eighth graders.

I pretend not to notice
when the bigger boys
pull Tyson
into a headlock,
rough him up,
call him worse names
than he calls me,
then whoop hysterically
like it's all fun and games.

When Tyson catches me
watching,
his face contorts.

I feel a pang of sympathy
but it's short-lived
because when he passes me
on his way off the bus,
he bumps my shoulder—hard—
and mutters
that he can't understand
how such a
       filthy
       pathetic
       loser
like me
has any friends
at all.

HYGIENE

Thankfully the school pool is not
full of rubber tires like my tub.

Or stacks of magazines
like Dad's shower.

Or located down a nearly impassable hallway
like our guest bathroom.

The pool and adjoining locker room
have a seemingly endless supply
of cool, clear water.

Which is important because
where else will I get clean?

LAUNDRY

As soon as
      I get home
          that afternoon
        I
    excavate
    a
  narrow
winding path
         through
           the basement
             praying I won't
                encounter any
                    of the critters
              I heard
          the night before.
      My hands shake
        as
          I
             unearth
             the
             washing machine
          and throw
          all my clothes
          inside
       hoping
      an extra cupful
      of detergent
will help wash
Tyson's
hurtful words
    away.

AWAY

There's no chapter in my orange book
about a grown-up who refuses to throw things   away.

There's no chapter in my orange book
about keeping your closest friends far   away.

Of course there isn't.

Because those aren't
worst-case scenarios
for anyone   normal.

CROSSING OVER

The next day
our unit on Arizona continues.
Ms. Treehorn places a map
on each of our desks.

It's just a piece of paper,
          innocent enough.

But I'm already feeling raw,
and this map
dredges up memories
I'd rather forget.

I trace my finger along
a jagged line.
Snaking somewhere
beneath the Colorado River
is the border
between Arizona and Nevada.

A single bridge staples
Bullhead City, Arizona, and Laughlin, Nevada,
together
along a swollen blue seam.

A lot of folks live in one city
and commute across the bridge
to work in the other.

Just like Mom used to do.

Crossing over
each day.

BORDERS

A tricky thing
about underwater
borders:

it's hard
to figure out
where one place
starts
and another
ends.

If something
happens

in the
murky
middle,

who's responsible?

BREACH

I raise my hand,
ask to see the nurse,
pretend
to have a stomachache.
      But really
I worry
if I look at this map
a minute longer,
my eyes may
      overflow
like the Colorado River
breaching its banks

∞ ∞ ∞

The school nurse
takes my temperature,
brings me some juice,
asks if I'd like to go home.

That's the last place
I want to go.

So I blame the cafeteria tuna salad,
tell the nurse I probably just need to rest.

She nods, closes
the plasticky curtain,
giving me privacy.

I curl up,
clutch my orange book.
My heart hammers my ribs.
I read
       chapter after chapter after chapter after chapter after
       chapter after chapter after chapter
                  until my nerves settle.

Worst-Case Scenario #320:
PIRANHAS

- Do not cross a piranha-infested river if you have an open wound, as they are attracted to blood.

- Avoid feeding areas such as fishing nets or docks.

- Cross the river at night.

- Swim or walk quietly.

- Disturb the water as little as possible.

- PROCEED WITH CAUTION!

WATER

At practice that afternoon,
I'm the first one
in the water.

Pick a cherry,
put it in your basket.
     One.

Pick a cherry,
put it in your basket.
     Two.

          Flip turn.
          Kick.

Pick a cherry,
put it in your basket.
     Three.

With each weightless lap
I feel better.
     Four.

Then worse.
     Five.

          Back and forth,
          through water

I hate and love
at the same time.

I tell Coach Baker
and Georgia and Liam
that my goggles
are cracked.

They believe
the chlorine made
my eyes so red.

UNIFORM

In preparation for our next swim meet,
Coach Baker hands out
team uniforms.

We're required
to wear the same
yellow swim caps and
embarrassingly small swim trunks
that are tight
in all the wrong places.
A brand called
Wave Makers.

Liam wiggles his butt, says,
More like
Wedgie Makers!

I might not be
in the mood
to laugh,
but I do smile,
and that helps.

TREASURES

Another sale at the Rummage Room? I ask back at home,
assessing the kitchen table, now officially buried.

A spectacular deal.
Too good to pass up!

Dad holds a crinkled receipt.
His fingers trace each number
like they give him
some kind of comfort
I cannot.

Thankfully tacos
have a similar effect.
So I propose dinner
at Miguel's.

Dad agrees,
as long as extra hot sauce
is part of the equation.

BACK TO LIFE

A strange thing happens
when Dad and I leave
our house.

No matter how weird
he's been acting,
the moment we step   outside
                                    away from
                                    the Hoard

my father comes back
        to life.

I enjoy this
while it lasts.
        (Which is never
        long enough.)

COLLIN VERSUS THE HOARD

Like the creepy creatures
in those movies Liam loves,
the Hoard has become
something alive,
consuming everything
in its path.

Each day
I steel myself for battle.
I clear new paths.
I excavate pockets
of precious air.

I push, shove, kick
piles of junk,
just trying to make
my way.

I begin to bury
my feelings
and memories
beneath the layers.

I think it may be easier
to survive this strange   After
if I forget
how life used to be   Before.

THIN ICE

I'm not the only one
with a fighting problem.

In the hallway between classes,
I overhear Principal Rodriguez
breaking up a brawl between
Liam and Tyson.
You boys are on thin ice, he says.

Liam chuckles.
That's a funny thing to say in the desert!

Principal Rodriguez isn't amused.
Detentions snowball into suspensions,
which snowball into expulsion.

Snowballs? Brrr . . . Tyson's voice is thick with attitude.

Mr. Herrera! Mr. Urvall! Enough!
What I'm saying is your current behavior
could affect your future.
Colleges don't look kindly
on a record of disruption
and disobedience.

College? That's like a million years from now,
Liam says.

Fine. Let me use a more immediate example:
three strikes and then
summer school.

T-MINUS 81

I'm not saying
I'm a super-nerd
or a teacher's pet
or one of those kids
who just loves every minute of school,
but being here *is* better
than hanging with the Hoard,
which is one of the reasons
Liam's summer countdown calendar
gives me serious heartburn.
        Or maybe it's all the tacos
        Dad and I have been eating?

Worst-Case Scenario #212:
INDIGESTION

- If you experience bloating, belching, nausea, or belly pain after eating, you may suffer from indigestion.

- Do not chew with your mouth open or eat too fast.

- This makes you swallow air, which can add to discomfort.

- Limit greasy, extra-sugary, or fried foods.

- Avoid spicy and acidic ingredients.

- Symptoms may be more intense when you're stressed.

- RELAX!

INCANDESCENT

On the day of our swim meet
I scan the bleachers,
packed with fans.

I'm so excited to see Dad
that I surprise myself
and Coach Baker
by actually winning
my backstroke event.

Way to go, bud! Dad cheers.
You are becoming increasingly hydrodynamic.
A fixed incandescent point in this natatorium.

Translation, dude? Liam whispers,
totally confused by the compliment.

I'm getting faster.
He called me a star of the pool.

Your dad always uses the weirdest words.

I know, I say, beaming.

> It's one of the reasons
> I love him.

SPLASH

A man wearing a hat
with a long silver fish on the front
is talking to Coach Baker.

When Georgia sees the scout,
she turns rigid as a pole.

I worry she'll trip and fall or
belly flop big-time.

But she climbs the ladder confidently,
steps onto the diving board,
lifts her chin.

Go, Gannet!
We clap
when she does her
front flip with a twist.

        She
        barely
        makes

            a
               S
               P
               L
               A
               S
               H
               !

SUITS

The health effects of
extended chlorine exposure
haven't been adequately studied,
so I err on the side of caution
and shower quickly but thoroughly
after swim meets and practices.

Though mostly
I'm grateful for the chance
to bathe somewhere other than
the grimy, cluttered bathrooms
at home.

Before leaving the locker room,
my teammates and I
hang our new race suits
on hooks in the locker room,
forming a row of practically identical
Wedgie Makers.

It would be easy
to mix them up.

I'll write my name
on the tag later.
Dad's waiting for me now.

SMALL VICTORIES

When the hostess at the restaurant
asks our name for the wait list,
Dad rattles off a bunch of letters
that do not spell Brey.

Ten minutes later
the intercom booms,
> *Communist, party of two!*
> *Now seating*
> *the Communist party!*

Dad's amusement is contagious.
By the time we land in the booth,
our stomachs ache
with laughter.

Over root-beer floats
as big as our faces,
we toast to my small victory
in the pool.

Then Dad dives in,
describing quantum mechanics
with the same enthusiasm
Coach Baker reserves for swim meets:
> intense eyes,
> wild hand gestures,
> occasional hollers.

When he doesn't notice
the vanilla ice cream
smeared across his bushy beard,
I hand him a napkin.

How embarrassing!
He grins, wiping his face clean.
Gee, bud,
what would I do
without you?

The waitress delivers our cheeseburgers
and asks if she can get us anything else.
Dad surveys the table.
A tomato-based condiment, please.
And the third largest city in North Dakota.

Pardon?

Hint: It's not Bismark
or Fargo!

She stares blankly at us.

We need ketchup
and some forks, please, I say,
stepping in as translator.

Yes! That's my boy!
Grand Forks it is!
Population 56,057.

The waitress sighs before setting some silverware
and a bottle of Heinz on the table.

So, bud, Dad says, spearing a pickle
with the third largest city in North Dakota.
We've been having heated debates

about mathematical space-time models at work.
I'm curious: what are your theories
regarding the origin and ultimate fate
of the universe?

He's 100 percent serious.
This is his idea
of casual dinner conversation.

I describe an article I read online
and tell him about an experiment we did
in science class, trying to connect
concepts I barely understand.

He nods, his eyes bright.

Away from the Hoard,
      unplugged
from his headphones,
he listens, lips quirked
in an eager smile.

Then he fills in the gaps
of my half-baked
explanations and observations
with shimmery specks of brilliance.
Somehow taking all the garbage
that tumbles out of my mouth
and constructing something
incredible.

Yes, I say.
That. Exactly.

Spectacular! he hoots,
jotting down notes and numbers
on a fresh napkin.
I wish I'd thought of that!
He scratches his chin.
Hey, bud . . .

Yeah, Dad?

You amaze me.
You really do.

Thanks, Dad.

If only I could perform
that same magic trick at home—
transform the Hoard
into something beautiful.
Something to make me feel
       proud
         and amazed.

Instead of
all the hard-to-name
emotions
I'm collecting
inside.

GOOD RIDDANCE

On Wednesday morning
an unexpected
ray of hope—
      Keith is moving to Seattle.

Ms. Treehorn throws a goodbye party,
wishes him good luck at his new school

Liam, Georgia, and I exchange glances
silently saying, *Good riddance!*
We toast paper cups of fruit punch,
celebrating
one less bully
to make our lives miserable.

Across the room,
Tyson's face
turns to stone,
cold and mean,
like a grumpy gargoyle.
Not even chocolate chip mini-muffins
cheer him up.

Worst-Case Scenario #119:
EARTHQUAKE

- If you are indoors when an earthquake strikes, take cover beneath a desk, table, or doorway.

- Stay clear of windows and gas lines.

- If you are outside, move to an open area, away from falling structures or debris.

- PREPARE FOR AFTERSHOCKS!

DOORBELL

Later that week
we play hockey
in Liam's living room
which is as different from mine
as imaginable,
with polished wood floors,
ample open space,
and a couch you can actually sit on.

Georgia stands in front
of the coffee table goal,
covered with makeshift padding
I insisted she wear for safety.

I feel like a human marshmallow! She giggles.

Well, you look like a sumo wrestler, Liam says.

Uhh, thanks?

I secure more pillows to her arms and legs
with bungee cords that Liam found
in a neatly organized utility closet.

The simple fact that he could easily locate them
is a miracle to me.

The hazard-free floor is another miracle.

So is Georgia's laugh.
I decide she has the second-best laugh in the world.
        (After Mom's, of course.)

TRASH TALK

Liam is a magnificent
trash-talker.
Want my autograph now or later?
They call me Matchstick 'cause I'm on FIRE!

Oh, really?
I heard Principal Rodriguez say you were on thin ice!

Shhh! You evil eavesdropper! He nabs the ball.

I chase, slash
his quick ankles.

Booya! Booya!
Send my fan mail to www-dot-Liam-rules-dot-com!
Crocodile mouth, armadillo butt!

What does that even mean?

Wouldn't you like to know! Ha-ha!

I'm mid–slap shot
when the doorbell
rings.

DOORBELL DREAD

We pause the game
to see who it is.
I hope it's not Georgia's dad,
coming to pick her up so soon.

Sharon walks down the hallway, yoga-calm.
She opens the front door
      not just a sliver,
      not a crack,
           W – I – D – E   O – P – E – N.

My pulse quickens,
my hands grow clammy
as I imagine
what would happen
if someone came to *my* house
      unannounced
and stuck their head
inside.

Oh. It's just Audrey from across the street, Liam tells us.
*Sometimes the mail carrier accidentally delivers
our packages to her house.
Come on. Let's get back to our game.*

I can feel Georgia watching me.
You okay? she asks,
her voice muffled
behind all those pillows.

Yeah. My mouth is dry,
my skin feels hot,
but I try to act cool.

*Are postal mix-ups included
in that handbook of yours?* she teases,
nudging my elbow.

Nah. I shake my head
and force a chuckle.

I make a mental note
to add *Uninvited Visitors*
to my growing list of
disasters worth preparing for.

When I get home, I'll inspect our locks and bolts.

∞ ∞ ∞

I wish I could stay
at Liam's house
all weekend,
with its clean floors,
home-cooked meals,
and open front door.

But Lindsay invited a bunch of her friends over,
and Liam warns me to get out
while I still can.

Save yourself! he cries, pretending to
gouge out his eyeballs.

If only I could
offer him refuge
from the incoming swarm of
      hair-tossing,
      lip gloss–smacking
      gossip-yappers.

∞ ∞ ∞

Before I leave
I let Liam flip through my orange book.

It's alphabetized by scenario, I tell him.

He says there must be a chapter missing between
      Gila monsters and
      Halitosis.

I double-check but
unfortunately
there's nothing in there about
      Girls.

Just like Uninvited Visitors,
lots of things in life
don't come with instructions.

Worst-Case Scenario #129:
GILA MONSTER

- Gila monsters are sluggish yet venomous.

- If you are bitten, remove the lizard as quickly as possible.

- Pry open the animal's mouth with a stick, knife, or other tool.

- Wash the wound with antibacterial soap.

- Call your local animal control and poison centers.

- Seek treatment at the nearest medical facility.

- Ensure your tetanus immunizations are up-to-date.

- Watch for signs of infection.

- There is no antivenin for Gila monster bites.

- BEWARE!

HEATSTROKE

I ride my bike home.
It's almost eighty degrees outside
and it's only February.

At this rate,
summer will be a
doozy.

After just five minutes,
I feel like I'm going to faint.
Thankfully the Henny Penny is only a block away.

I sip from the drinking fountain,
then browse the air-conditioned aisles
for almost an hour,
until Mrs. Finnick tells me to stop loitering
and get lost.

∞ ∞ ∞

By the bike rack
my ears ring.

I swear I hear:
>   *Filthy.*
>   *Pathetic.*
>   *Loser.*

My book says
dizziness and confusion

are symptoms of heatstroke,
so I visit the fountain one last time.

> *Filthy!*
> *Pathetic!*
> *Loser!*

I lift my head,
wipe water from my lips.
I see Tyson (minus his usual sidekick),
        sluggish, venomous,
snickering by the shopping cart corral.

I jump back on my bike.

At least the blazing heat
stops him
from chasing me.

SMELLS

Ms. Treehorn told us
one's sense of smell
is most closely linked
to memory.

She's probably right,
because whenever I'm at the Henny Penny
and I get a whiff
      of jasmine
      or licorice
      or rubbing alcohol
my skin gets prickly.

For one teensy
tiny
second
I think maybe,
      just maybe,
Mom is in the next aisle over
buying more of that lotion
      that made her hands soft as flower petals.
Or nibbling jelly beans from the candy counter,
      the black ones that no one else ever buys.
Or picking up groceries after work,
      that clean-hospital smell lingering on her clothes.

NEW SMELLS

There's a reason
perfumes don't contain
notes of
        unwashed laundry,
        soured milk,
        musty mildew,
        stewed garbage,
        thousand-year-old burrito.

These are the smells
that have replaced
        jasmine and licorice and rubbing alcohol.

These are the smells that
assault me, remind me
day after day
that the Hoard
is winning.

That Tyson
is right
about me.

Worst-Case Scenario #180:
HEATSTROKE

- The symptoms of heatstroke include core body temperature above 104°F, fainting, headache, dizziness, rapid heartbeat, and muscle weakness.

- If you suspect you may be suffering from severe heatstroke, immediately seek medical help. In the meantime, move to an air-conditioned environment or shady area.

- Reduce all physical activity. Drink plenty of fluids.

- Remove any heavy, tight, or unnecessary clothing.

- Cool off with cold compresses, showers, or baths.

- CHILL OUT!

T-MINUS 73

On Valentine's Day
everyone acts
gushy, mushy, weird.

Ms. Treehorn gives us
bright pink candies
that taste like chalk.

At least they're not
GrossBombs.

I wish she'd give us
cinnamon hearts instead,
the extra fiery ones
that burn you up
in a good way.

The chalk candies say
cheesy stuff like:
> Be Mine
> U R Special 2 Me
> Smothered w. Love

Who would ever want to be
> smothered
> with love?

That sounds terrible.

GILA BREATH

In an act of total insanity
Tyson tries to kiss Sabrina
at recess.

She slaps his face so hard
a bright red handprint appears.
Nice try, Gila Breath!
Snowflake's chance in Bullhead
I'd let your lips near mine!

For once I'm grateful
for Sabrina's loud mouth.

I really hope Tyson learns
that what he did
is not okay.
I also hope
his new nickname
sticks.

It might be
even worse
than mine.

CRAZY

I let Liam have my candy hearts.
He shakes his head, says,
*Love makes people act
all kinds of crazy.*

*For a bullheaded knucklehead,
you have moments
of surprising wisdom,* I say.

*People always underestimate the funny guy.
But I have, like, Yoda-level wisdom.*

And so humble are you.

*I'm wiser than Gila Breath, that's for sure.
Trying to smooch a girl? Ugh.
What was he thinking?*
Liam gobbles a huge handful of candy.
I'm clearly wiser than you, too, Worst-Case Collin.

Oh, really, Matchstick?

*Yup. Giving up candy?
That's crazy all right.
You* must *realllllly love me.*

Sure. I laugh.
*I love you
like I love
stepping on a tack.*

*Ha! Well, my brother-from-another-mother,
I love you*

like I love
ants in my sandwich.

I love you
like I love
itching powder
in my underwear.

Guys? Really?
Enough with the bromancing, Georgia says,
grabbing the last few hearts.

Jealous Gannet is, Liam croaks in his best Yoda voice.

Georgia rolls her eyes,
but her cheeks suddenly flush
as pink as the candies in her hand.

KISSING

I've never thought much about
kissing a girl.

If I ever do,
it might not be
so bad
to think about
kissing
Georgia.

Worst-Case Scenario #178:
HALITOSIS

- To prevent bad breath, avoid garlic, onions, and other odor-causing foods.

- Brush your teeth twice a day with fluoride toothpaste.

- Don't forget to brush your tongue, too.

- Use floss to remove food particles and plaque.

- Rinse with mouthwash.

- See your dentist regularly.

- If halitosis persists, use chewing gum or mints to mask unpleasant odors.

- PUCKER UP!

EVERYTHING

Did you ever buy Mom flowers on Valentine's Day?
Or chocolates, or anything like that? I ask Dad at dinner,
missing her always,
not just on crazy-making days
devoted to love.

Dad pauses, his spoon spilling
minestrone soup back into his bowl.
I did. She liked sunflowers best.
He sets his spoon down, takes a breath.
Your mother was everything to me.
When we lost her . . .
When she . . .

Across the restaurant table
I see a turtle tucking
into its dark, thick shell.

I don't ask any more questions.

I'm too afraid
of losing him, too.

EVERYTHING AND NOTHING

Back at home
I examine
the expanding, thriving
Hoard.

I think I might be having
one of those eureka moments:

>Dad lost his everything.

>Now he has
>every
>>*thing*.

Wait.
If Mom was everything,

>what am I?

T-MINUS 68

Ms. Treehorn launches into a new lesson
about Arizona's unique flora and fauna.

Any coincidence flora rhymes with BORE-ah?
Liam mutters.

I ignore him
because plants remind me
of Mom.

Some days, thinking about her
feels like tumbling down
a cactus-covered hillside—
        something most people
        would try to avoid.

But lately
I just want to remember
(even if it stings a little bit).

OCOTILLO

Ms. Treehorn flicks the projector on.
Ocotillo plants are mostly leafless,
except immediately after it rains,
when they suddenly burst bright.
After the soil dries again,
the leaves wither quickly.

Each time she says
oh–koh–tee–yo
the word dashes out of her mouth
                    like a flat stone
                              skipping rings
                                    across water.

Too bad people have given it
dumb nicknames like:
          Coachwhip
          Flaming Sword
          Jacob's Staff

Well, I guess Flaming Sword is pretty cool.

MOVIE NIGHT

When the weekend rolls around,
I make up excuses about
>a malfunctioning air-conditioning unit,
>a neighbor's irritating Chihuahua,
>a telemarketer that calls nonstop.

So we go to Georgia's house
for peace and quiet and movies
instead of mine.

Liam chooses the video.
Georgia makes the snacks.

What should I bring? I ask.

An alien invasion preparation plan.

That I can do, I say, waving my orange book.

We sit on giant beanbags
in Georgia's living room
stuffing our faces
with popcorn.
We throw kernels at Liam,
teasing him ruthlessly
about his terrible taste
in movies.

This one is called
>*Space Invaders*
another cheesy sci-fi
that's more silly
than scary.

After the movie,
I go to Liam's house
for a sleepover.

Sharon drives me home
the next morning.

At each intersection
her eyes flit
to the rearview mirror.

Her eyebrows form
a tight line.

I pretend not to notice her
noticing me.

Oh, babe, she says
when she pulls up to my house.

My eyes dart
to the door—
        to make sure
        it's closed.

It's such a sunny day.
Pity to have the curtains drawn like that.
Tell your dad he ought to let a little light in.

I will, I say.
Thanks for the ride.

I jump out of the minivan
before Liam has a chance
to ask about coming over.

Before the Hoard forces me
to tell more lies and make
more awful excuses.

SPACE INVADER

I discover
my bedroom door
          O P E N.

No! No! No!
There is so
so
so
so
much
stuff
      invading
      my
      space!

RESTORED

Fuming, I remove
    yellowed newsprint,
    faded magazines,
    bins of dusty garden supplies.

I sort the clothes
piled on my bed.
Most are wool sweaters
that promise nothing
but itch and sweat.

I find a pair of cargo shorts and
a few new T-shirts in my size.
I slip them into my dresser.

I wipe down my desk,
dust my shelves.

I bag and drag
the remaining stuff
into the hallway,
until my refuge is
restored.

But I'm not satisfied;
I'm angry.
This single square
of space
is not nearly
enough.

HOW I FEEL AT HOME

junk junk junk garbage garbage garbage stuff stuff stuff junk
junk junk garbage garbage garbage stuff stuff stuff junk junk
junk garbage garbage garbage stuff stuff stuff junk junk junk
garbage garbage garbage stuff stuff stuff junk junk junk garbage
garbage garbage stuff stuff stuff junk junk junk junk garbage
stuff garbage garbage stuff stuff stuff junk junk junk garbage
garbage garbage stuff stuff stuff junk junk junk garbage garbage
garbage stuff stuff stuff junk junk junk garbage garbage garbage
stuff stuff stuff junk junk junk garbage garbage garbage stuff
stuff stuff junk junk junk garbage garbage garbage stuff stuff
stuff junk junk junk garbage garbage garbage stuff stuff stuff
junk junk junk garbage garbage   stuff stuff junk
junk junk junk garbage garba   ME   arbage garbage
garbage garbage junk junk gar   ME   arbage garbage
junk stuff junk stuff stuff garbag   rbage stuff stuff
stuff junk junk junk garbage gar   stuff stuff stuff
junk junk junk garbage garbage garbage stuff stuff stuff junk
junk junk garbage garbage garbage stuff stuff stuff junk junk
junk garbage garbage garbage stuff stuff stuff junk junk junk?

144

CLEAR

I ride until
      my mind
            clears.

Legs pump,
      wheels
            turn.

Slowly
      sidewalk
            dissolves.

Houses,
      streetlights,
            stop signs

fade
      into the
            background.

My lungs
      fill with
            unshared air.

BOUNDARIES

A chain-link fence has sprouted around the vacant lot, declaring new borders. Making the desert less wild than it should be.

Or is someone trying to keep something else in?

Is someone trying to keep me out?

TRIM

Hey, Shaggy Maggy.
Nice hair!
Tyson's voice rattles off metal lockers
the next day at school.

Everyone turns to
stare.

Shut your piehole, Gila Breath! Liam snaps.

Mind your business, Loser Face!

Tyson's such a jerk,
but I haven't had a trim in months.
and it *is* getting harder
to stuff all that hair
into my swim cap.

CHALLENGE

Is everything okay? Georgia asks at lunch.

Yeah. Sure. Why? I reply as casually as possible,
wondering why my face always gives away
truths I'd rather keep hidden.

You're acting funky lately, Liam says, scratching his head.

Funky, like, cool? I flash the world's most awkward jazz hands.

Definitely not like that. Never do that again.
Whatever that was. Liam shudders.

Well, there is one thing
I can share with my friends.
When Keith moved
I thought things would be half as bad.
But Tyson's become twice as mean.

You're right, Georgia says, taking a bite of her veggie wrap.
I noticed the same thing.

Liam scratches his head some more.

You got lice in there or something? I ask, inching away from him.
My book has a whole chapter about those . . .

Nope. I've got an idea.
A real itchy one.

It's called thinking, Liam. Georgia rolls her eyes.

I know. I may be allergic.

That would explain a lot. She laughs.

Are you plotting some bonkers prank
to put Tyson in his place, once and for all? I ask,
recalling the names he called me earlier,
embarrassing me in front of the whole class. Again.

No, but that's an interesting idea . . .
Liam studies me from across the table.
This is about you, Worst-Case Collin.

My stomach twists.
Does it have anything to do with my shaggy hair?

No, no. He waves his hand dismissively.
I bet I can beat you at butterfly, he declares.

I sigh with relief,
glad the conversation has shifted.
I bet you can't, I say.
His stroke is a Gatorade-snort-worthy disaster.

Let's let the clock decide.
Today. Before practice.

What's at stake, Matchstick? I grin, my mood lifting.
Like Dad, I have a hard time resisting a good challenge.

If I win, you play Candy Roulette.

Fine. When I win, you stop calling me Worst-Case Collin.

Challenge accepted!

TSUNAMI

Ready to lose? I say, splashing Liam.
He didn't even warm up.
Rookie mistake.

Hope you're hungry,
'cause you're about to eat my wake!
Liam smiles deviously.

You know what happens to matchsticks in water, right? I reply.
They fizzle out!

Georgia yells,
Ready, set, go!

I push off the block.
      Each kick
            threads me through
           smooth water.
                  I pull closer, closer
                      to the wall,
                      confident, strong.

Then, out of the corner
of my goggles—
      a tsunami!
Liam's caught
in the wave.
His legs flailing,
fighting,
like I've never seen before.

My rescue instinct goes into
overdrive.

I will not let my friend drown!

I thrash wildly
in his direction.

Then I see his head pop
up to the surface,
          breathe,
flail,
swish,
          breathe.

He's not drowning at all.
He's beating me.

Now it's my competitive instinct
in overdrive.

          I will not let that sandbagging showboat win!

I rip across the lane
          trying to catch
          and match
                    his wacky stroke.

My muscles screech.
I swear someone
dropped
a piano
on my back.
I am
          sinking.

Liam's fingers touch the wall
full, fat seconds
before mine.

I sputter,
burning lungs
coughing chlorine.

Georgia confirms the win,
shaking her head in disbelief.

Liam pulls himself out of pool,
tugs his swimsuit,
sprints gracelessly
to the locker room
without a word.

In all the years
I've known him,
he's never run away
from winning
   without doing some obnoxious victory dance.

Something is seriously wrong.

VOCABULARY

Skullduggery: sneaky, tricky, dishonest behavior;
AKA filling your opponent's Wedgie Maker with itching
powder.

Numbskullery: stupid, dumb, foolish (but really freaking
funny) behavior;
AKA accidentally filling *your own* Wedgie Maker with itching
powder.
See also: Liam Edward Urvall

CANDY ROULETTE

Once Liam showers and recovers
from the irksome itch
of his own numbskullery,
our bet is not forgotten.

Make a choice.
Your fate is in your hands, he says,
mischief flickering in his eyes.
He holds a round red candy in each palm:
  one GrossBomb,
  one Fireball.

It's in your hands, technically, I say, shaking my head.

Make your selection wisely, Worst-Case Collin.
You must live with the consequences, he taunts.
For a full three minutes, okay?
No cheating. No spitting.

He enjoys this way too much, I say.

Seriously. Georgia sighs.
Liam, if you spent half as much time on your homework
as you spend devising these schemes,
I'm pretty sure you wouldn't be
three strikes away from summer school.

True.
But school is so much less fun
than torturing you fools!
Mwahahaha!

How do I know this isn't rigged? I ask.

He gawks, offended.
*Do I really look like the type of scoundrel
who would scam his best friend?*

Yes! Georgia and I say in unison.

What? The swimsuit mix-up was a happy accident!

Don't worry, Georgia says to me under her breath.
I ran quality control.

I squint.
The candies are identical,
except one promises brief pain followed by sweetness.
The other, the opposite.

Remind me why I agreed to this?

You lost a bet, Liam replies smugly.

*For the record, it's a contested win
marred by controversy and skullduggery.*

*Dude, you sound way too much like your dad
when you use big words like that.
You lost. Deal with it.*

I'd rather lick the scuzz off the locker-room floor
than eat another GrossBomb.
But a bet is a bet.

I lean closer.

Hey! No sniffing allowed! he shouts

Fine.
I grab the candy from his left hand.
My mouth waters.

Cinnamon flames engulf my tongue.
I display the Fireball between my teeth,
pulling my lips into a tingly, victorious smile.

Liam looks disappointed.
Georgia looks pleased.
Too pleased.

Did she perform some act of skullduggery
for me?

The thought sends a funny warmth
through my chest and into my belly.

Or maybe
that's just the cinnamon.

BAD IDEAS

At the vacant lot
posters announce:
> *New shopping mall*
> *coming soon!*

I think this is
a bad idea
because shovels will disturb
the ground.

A bad idea
because giant blocky buildings
will crowd
the sky.

A bad idea
because new stores
will entice Dad
to buy more crap
we don't need,
with money
we don't have.

A bad idea
because I'll have one less
safe place.

HALT

Apparently I'm not the only one
who thinks the shopping mall
is a very bad idea.

The next day
protesters flood the site.
They carry signs,
shouting,
> *Preservation!*
Demanding,
> *Proper excavation!*

By the end of the week,
construction halts.

CHURN

I find Dad
hunched in the shadows
of his room
churning through stuff.

I navigate
piles of junk
wondering why
we need crates
of wire clothes hangers,
bent and twisted
like metal spiders wrestling.
Or dozens of boots
with no matches,
in sizes neither of us wears.

I tiptoe
      high-step
over
      each obstacle.

When I finally
reach him,
I tap his shoulder.

He jumps,
yanks the headphones off.
Hey, bud.

Dad, I need a haircut.

He looks annoyed.
I'm distracting him

from something
important.

I stare at the pages
spread across his bed,
expecting to find
      scientific data sheets,
      academic journals,
      the Riemann hypothesis—solved!

Instead
I see catalogs and flyers
advertising deals for things
that will not help
      explain the universe,
      cure rare diseases,
      solve a math equation,

      or give a boy
      a haircut.

∞ ∞ ∞

He tells me to look
in his bathroom
for some clippers
to cut my own hair.

He's too busy
to take me to the barber shop.

The papers,
the deals,
the junk,

all more important
than me.

I suddenly want to light a match
and burn everything.

I take a few deep breaths
and decide burning down the house
is not a good idea.

Other bad ideas include
        cutting my own hair.

I'm pretty sure
I'd cause irreparable damage
to my head.

But maybe
if I find the clippers,
Georgia will agree
to help me.

∞ ∞ ∞

The bathroom smells
swampy.

Constellations of mold
splotch the ceiling.

Soggy magazines
look bruised and beaten,
ink bleeding
blue, black, green

on the floor.

Bottles and jars
crowd the countertop.

The faucet cries endlessly,
one drip-drop tear
at a time.

If I weren't so red-hot mad,
my eyes might
do the same.

∞ ∞ ∞

Inside the first drawer
I find five crusty tubes of toothpaste.

Mom's old makeup
is in the second drawer,
including that sticky
smooch-attack lipstick
that should have been
thrown away
long ago.

I twist the cap, but the pink shade
looks ghoulish in this light,
nothing like the color
of Mom's real smile.

I jump back
when I open the third drawer.

This brown furry thing
isn't a rodent,
but it's still disturbing.

It's one of Dad's bizarro collections:
      tufts of hair
      trimmed from his beard
      and his head
      (and I hope nowhere else).

The clippers
may be hiding
at the bottom,
but I sure as heck
won't reach my hand in
to find out.

I open the final drawer.
It's even grosser
than the last,
scattered with a thousand
pale-yellow crescents.
More clippings:
      fingernails;
      toenails, too.

I slam the drawer shut.

I want to run
        OUT
        of this room
        of this house
        of this life
            as fast as I can!

Instead
the Hoard forces me
to climb
over jagged mountains
of garbage,
while I scream a silent river
                of the biggest, baddest words

                                inside my head.

BORDERLESS

I escape into nature,
seeking wide-open spaces
where I can
breathe.

I venture beyond the vacant lot,
leaving its chain-link boundaries
behind.

My shadow s t r e t c h e s
as the sun arcs.
A few tumbleweeds
roll past, as aimless and lost
as I feel.

I look up, squint,
search the sky
for answers.

Mom and I used to play a game
spotting shapes and patterns
in the clouds,
spinning stories about their meaning,
like fortune-tellers reading tea leaves.

Today the clouds are stubborn;
they don't tell me much
about the future.

At least they help me
remember
the past.

PERFECT

I'm sure there were times
> when Mom acted grouchy after a long shift at
>> the hospital,
> when she made me wear something mortifyingly dorky
>> to a family function,
> when she cooked something revoltingly healthy like
>> kale casserole for dinner.

The logical part of my brain knows
no one is perfect.
> Not even Mom.

But my heart refuses to believe it.
Or, at the very least,
it won't let me remember
anything but the good stuff.

And right now
I'm fine with that.

LEAVING

I can't help but wonder
if Mom hadn't left us
the way she did—
      too soon,
      without a choice—
would she leave us
      now?

Would the Hoard
push her
      over the edge?

Would it take her
      away?

Would she choose
      to go?

            No, because if she were
              still here,
         the Hoard would never
            have grown.
           She would have kept
             the beast
              at bay.

Worst-Case Scenario #226:
JAMMED DOOR

- If you need to enter a room, try to open the door by turning the knob.

- If that doesn't work, locate tools to remove the lockset from the door.

- If there is no time to unscrew the hardware, use a heavy, solid object to strike the hinges until they break.

- Kick the door at its weakest point.

- Run at the door, slamming it with your shoulder again and again until it opens.

- KEEP TRYING!

NEST

The next day after school,
Georgia cuts my hair
in a shady spot outside the gym
with scissors borrowed
from the sixth-grade craft closet.

When I ask her to be careful
        not to chop off my ears,
        or accidentally stab herself with the shears,
        or give me some hideous style like a mullet,
she takes a deep breath and shares
her grandmother's favorite Chinese proverb:
That the birds of worry
fly over your head,
this you cannot change.
But that they build nests in your hair,
this you can prevent.

It takes a few minutes
for this idea to sink in,
but as it does, I feel better.

I won't save the clippings
the way Dad does,
in a creepy drawer of secrets.

Instead
I let them fall to the ground
for some bird
to pick up
and build a nest with
        elsewhere.

Georgia chatters about diving
while she tries to tame
my overgrown mane.

I let her voice,
      her laugh,
           carry me
                far away.

Only the top divers and swimmers in the state
train at Camp Barracuda, she tells me,
snipping the last few strands.
Now close your eyes.
She places something on my head.
Much better. Open!

She holds up a round pocket mirror.

In it, I see my reflection
wearing a hat
with a long silver fish on the front.

What's this?

A barracuda! she squeals.
I've been invited to join their summer dive team!

I'm so happy for her.

Until I realize it means
she'll be gone
all summer,
hours away
from Bullhead City.

I feel bad
wishing
she would stay.

Mostly I wish
I were a faster swimmer
or a better diver
so I could go, too.

3

Georgia, Liam, me.
Together
we are three.

A prime number,
indivisible,
because nothing can
break us apart.

Except maybe swim camp.
Or summer school.
And possibly the Hoard.

GIVING

Your protein filaments look good, Dad says,
standing in my doorway that evening.

Huh? Oh. You mean my hair?

He nods.
*I'm sorry I couldn't take you
to the barber shop the other day, bud.
I want to make it up to you.*

My heart jumps,
hoping he'll suggest
      root-beer floats at the diner,
      a game of mini-golf,
      anything for us to do together
          away from the Hoard

Or, even better,
maybe he's finally decided to clean up a little . . .

He disappears for a second,
then returns
heaving a giant bag
into my room.

What's this? I peek inside
at an assortment of outdated electronics.

*For you, bud.
I'm sure there are treasures
in there somewhere!*

I run my fingers through
my newly cut hair,
trying to hide
my disappointment.

He has good intentions, but
my father keeps giving me
stuff
that I don't need
or want.

SPACE AND TIME

I persuade Dad to take me to Miguel's.
At dinner his favorite topic of conversation is
the space-time continuum.

This is interesting because

space
       and
              time

are the only two
things
I actually wish
he would give me.

I just don't know
how to tell him that.

EQUATIONS

While we wait for our meal,
I slide a sheet of paper
across the table.
It's a selfish diversion,
but I know Dad won't mind.

He smacks his lips,
rubs his palms together,
like checking my math homework
is more scrumptious than
the towering platter of nachos
we just ordered.

*The last few equations are
completely impossible,* I say.

Those are the best sort!

*No, really. Ms. Treehorn must've forgotten
to give us some of the information.*

Dad studies the page.
Not so! He beams.
*Fun math problems
usually have a lot of unknowns.*

I generally think *fun* and *math*
don't belong in the same sentence.

I guess that just proves
how different
we really are.

UNKNOWNS

The nachos arrive.
Dad's half of the plate
grows cold
as he tries to explain
$X + Y = Z$

If you know X,
you can figure out Z,
and then you'll know Y.

But no matter how much
I study my father,
I cannot figure out
why.

WHY

Why is Dad one person
here
              and
why
is he so different
at home?

Why
can't someone
so smart
              understand?

Why
can't someone
with such gigantic eyeglasses
              see

what he's doing
to our house?

What he's doing
to me?

T-MINUS 62

Spring break is less than two weeks away.
When I remind Dad of this,
he looks at me with surprise and disbelief,
as if I just told him
that brown cows make chocolate milk.

Maybe I can come to work with you? I suggest,
dreading a week at home with the Hoard.

He shakes his head,
says he has too much to do.
He's developing a new syllabus
for summer courses.

Summer courses?
You never teach in the summer, I say.

It's a spectacular opportunity.
Too good to pass up.
Plus we need the money, bud.

My heart sinks.

∞ ∞ ∞

A few days later,
Sharon invites me to stay over
at their house for spring break.

I'm so happy,
I could cry.

Of course I don't
because Liam would tease me nonstop
for the entire week
and probably for all of eternity.
    I still want a new nickname but
    Crybaby Collin is not what I have in mind.

Instead, I do my best end zone victory dance
and karate chop the Hoard
on my way out the door.

Worst-Case Scenario #741:
TYPHOON

- To prepare for a typhoon, assemble an emergency kit with flashlights, batteries, medical supplies, and food.

- Fill the bathtub and other large containers with fresh water.

- Make a family communication plan.

- Cover your windows with plywood or storm shutters.

- Bring in all outdoor furniture and decorations.

- Stay inside during the storm.

- Keep away from windows and glass doors.

- Do not be fooled by a lull—it could be the eye of the storm—winds will pick up again!

- If the storm is too severe to shelter in place,

- EVACUATE!

PEACE OFFERING

Yo, Shaggy Maggy!
Tyson yanks my hair in the lunch line.
Your locks are gone
but you still reek like a freak!

Jax and his eighth-grade buddies
sit at a picnic table nearby,
egging Tyson on.

He calls me more names,
trying to make himself look **BIG**
by making me feel
small.

The only things that stink
are your jokes, Liam says, stepping beside me.

Someone makes a sizzling sound,
because Tyson just got burned!

Jax shakes his head,
like his little bro's suddenly nothing
but a big disappointment.

Liam, it's not polite
to make fun of someone's intelligence,
or lackluster sense of humor, says Georgia.

Liam whips around,
blink, blink, blinking.

Georgia strides forward,
her long braid swaying as she moves.

Sorry about that, she says,
flashing a sympathetic smile.

Now Tyson and Jax
blink, blink, blink
at Georgia.

Here. An open palm.
One round red candy.
Truce? she says oh-so-sweetly.

Tyson's slow bully brain
tries to process
what's happening.

His older stepbrother shrugs,
gives a nod of approval.
Tyson reaches out
to accept
the unexpected peace offering.

TRAITOR

Seriously? What was that all about? Liam snorts.

Georgia doesn't answer.
She just walks over to the swings,
smiling.

Her legs pump
                                    out
and in.

Seriously? Liam asks again,
turning to me.

He thinks Georgia's a traitor.
But I know better.

Sweet revenge, I say,
pointing across the field,
where Tyson folds in half,
grabbing his guts,
spitting a slobbery GrossBomb
into dry grass
while a circle of kids
laughs and jeers.

SHOW-AND-TELL

Ms. Treehorn asks us to bring something
meaningful to class
and explain its importance.

I'm pretty sure show-and-tell
is for kindergartners,
yet my classmates gladly share
      ballet slippers,
      stamp collections,
      action figures.

I squirm in my seat,
wondering if Liam has shaken
some of that itching powder
down my pants.

Sabrina holds up a backpack
with a metal frame and thick straps.
It's not what I expected her to bring at all.

I used this last summer
to hike the Bradshaw Mountains, she says.

It's hard to picture Sabrina hiking;
she usually acts so prissy.
But when she heaves the pack over her shoulder,
we all see a different side of her.

I had to carry everything on my back.
I could only bring essentials.

What a fantastic adventure!
How long was your trek? Ms. Treehorn asks.

One week.
When I get older, I'm going to backpack across Europe.
Like my parents did.
They traveled with one bag each for six months.

Only one? Really?

Yes, ma'am.
Dad says it was liberating.
Mom calls it the best decision of her life.
Until she had me, obviously.

Eventually we move on to the next student,
        but I'm stuck on that backpack.

Hiking in the mountains is rife
with innumerable dangers,
yet I keep imagining
the freedom and
possibility
of carrying hardly
any things
at all.

MY TURN

At the last minute,
I change my mind.

Instead of my original item,
I open the orange book
and read a chapter
out loud.

Everyone laughs
when they should be
paying attention.

Worst-Case Scenario #1003:
ZOMBIES

- To stop a zombie attack, shoot the flesh-eating, brain-munching, undead ghouls directly in the head.

- As an added precaution, burn the bodies.

- If that fails, collect food, water, and other necessities.

- Seek refuge. Hunker down.

- HIDE!

FOSSILS

Ms. Treehorn holds up
a curved stone.
Now it's my turn.
Can anyone guess what this is?

A very small armadillo? I venture.

Not quite.
Look closer.

She passes it to me.
I study the tiny armored creature
trapped between
layers of hardened silt and clay.

It's a fossil, obviously, Sabrina says,
grabbing it from my hands.

Indeed!
A marine trilobite
found not too far from here.

There's no ocean around here! Sabrina balks.

Not anymore, Ms. Treehorn says.
But there used to be.

In the desert? Really? I ask.

Yes. Time has a way of making
big changes.
About 520 million years ago,

Arizona was home to a shallow sea
that created many of the sedimentary rock formations
visible in our nearby canyons.
The archaeologist who gave me this says
trilobite fossils are quite common in these parts.

What makes it special
if it's so common? Sabrina asks.

Ms. Treehorn's face turns
ocotillo red.
I suppose it's special
because it reminds me
of someone special.

STRIKE ONE

Swim practice is cancelled,
even though we really need
to train for our upcoming meet.

Liam's stuck in detention
for putting a chocolate bar
that looked like a turd
in the pool.

He didn't want to swim extra laps today.

He's a real knucklehead sometimes.

But he's never afraid
to act.

SECRET

Georgia and I sit
in a sliver of shade
underneath
the basketball hoop,
watching heat
rise off the blacktop.

It's quiet when it's
just the two of us.

Quiet, but not
awkward.

If you have a secret,
you should tell it, Georgia says,
out of nowhere.

I grip the basketball
as hard as I can.
I'm afraid
it'll slip away.
My palms are sweating
that badly.

You should tell your secret
to someone you trust, she adds.

What does she know?
What does she suspect?

I wish I could tell her
what's really going on in my life,

but the worst-case scenarios
running through my head
roar and rumble,
keeping me quiet.

I already lost my mom.
I can't lose
my friends, too.

My fingertips follow
rubber lines
across the ball's bumpy orange skin,
wishing it were a globe
with a path to follow
out.

∞ ∞ ∞

I lied at show-and-tell, Georgia says.

I look at her,
puzzled.

That blanket my mom knit?
I didn't get it the day I was born.
I got it when I was seven months old.

Okay, I say.
That doesn't seem criminal.
Why'd you lie?

Collin,
my mom wasn't there
when I was born.

Georgia,
isn't that scientifically impossible?

Not if you're
adopted.

Oh.

That's my secret.

She doesn't ask for mine.
She might not even know
I have one.

∞ ∞ ∞

My fingers relax.
The ball rolls free.

I wish I could hold her hand
but my palms are too sweaty.

So I just look at her eyes,
which are looking at her shoes,
staring so hard,
blinking so fiercely,
like she's trying to fix
the untied laces with her mind,
in a feat of remarkable telekinesis.

I hate
that I don't know
what to say.

Lately my dumb book
seems no good for anything.

Some days I wonder why, she says quietly.

I try to help Georgia by
making questions become answers.
What if your birth parents couldn't take care of you?
What if they wanted more for you?
What if . . . ?

She scuffs her sneaker
on the ground.

My head spins,
like that hotshot trick
Liam can do,
with the basketball
balanced on his fingertip.

Don't get me wrong, she says.
I'm happy.
And lucky.
Still . . .

She turns to me.
Some days
I feel like
a throwaway.

My heart seizes up.

My father never throws
anything
away.

Especially not people.
Living people, dead people.
He keeps us all.

In spite of the weird, cluttered
life we live,
it's one of the reasons
I love him.

I lean over Georgia's foot
and tie her laces into
a looping tight
double knot.

It is a small thing to do,
but I can't find any words,
and I need her to know
I'll do what I can
to keep her
from falling.

To keep her
from getting hurt.

Because she's not
a throwaway to me.

When I finish the bow
that looks like a floppy
sideways infinite number eight,
she cups one of her hands
over mine.

She doesn't seem to mind
that it's sweaty and gross.

I knew you were
the right person
to tell.
If you ever need
to tell me something,
I'm here, Collin. Okay?

∞ ∞ ∞

We walk toward the bike rack,
both of us looking up
at the cloudless, uncluttered sky.

Georgia says,
I wish I could've met her.

I think she must be talking
about her birth mom.

Turns out
she's talking about
mine.

PHOTOGRAPHS

I reach into my backpack,
pull out the handful of
memories
I couldn't bear to share
at show-and-tell.

Now the time feels right.

Georgia studies them
with serious eyes.

She holds each glossy rectangle
with careful fingers.

She lifts my favorite photograph
up to the light.

Tell me about this one, she says,
like an archaeologist gently
      chip-chip-chipping
      hard stone,
          dust-dust-dusting
          layers of dirt
             from a fossil
             that's been trapped
             for too long.

She is so beautiful, Georgia says.
She has the best smile.

She also had the best laugh, I say,
describing the things
a photograph can't.

Your dad still has those glasses.
And those vests!
So many crazy vests!
Where does he find them?

The Rummage Room.
I laugh, even though it's not really funny.

Liam looks the same.
Only now he's bigger
and goofier.

And more annoying, I say.

Georgia picks up another photo:
  Mom and me together
  in the garden,
  squinting into the sun.
  Happy.

Wow, Collin. You look . . .

I wait and wait.

So much like her.
You have exactly
the same smile.

STAY

I stay behind at school,
making up some story
about an extra-credit assignment,
when really
I have nowhere else to go.

> The pool is being shocked.
> Georgia has a dentist appointment.
> Liam's in detention.

> Even the Henny Penny is off limits.
> Mrs. Finnick told me to quit spooking her customers,
> haunting the aisles,
> never buying so much as a jelly bean.

> Besides, Tyson likes to hang around there.
> The only thing I need less than a bag of broken
> electronics
> is trouble from him.

The janitor finishes cleaning the floors.
The hallway smells like lemons and bleach.

I watch him return his mop to the closet
and wave goodbye.

I'm alone.

Or so I think.

SO CLEVER

You think you and your dork squad
are so clever, don't you?
Humiliating me in front of Jax and all his friends?

I wheel around, stumble back.
Tyson's eyes burn with anger.

Getting your freckle-faced girlfriend to do your dirty work, huh?
Did you really think you'd get away with a stunt like that?
The only thing nastier than those prank candies is YOU!

A split second later,
I'm staring at the green flecks
in the linoleum
again.

Except this time
no one's around
to help.

Filthy!
      Pathetic!
Loser!

Slam!
      Pound!
Punch!

Now there are little red spots
all over the freshly mopped floor.

STAND UP

Georgia forgot something
in her locker.

When she comes back to get it,
she finds me.

*Why don't you ever
stand up for yourself?*
Her eyes are wet.
We should tell someone, she says.

I shake my head. *No.*
I don't want to bring
any extra attention
to my life.

I also don't want
Georgia to ruin
her special blanket,
but she dabs my bloody lip
with the frayed corner anyway.

*You can't let Tyson
do this to you, Collin.*

I want to tell her
      it's hard to argue
      against words
      you think
      might actually
      be true.

ONE MORE SECRET

Mr. Wolcott drives me home.
Georgia's dad is a really nice guy.
I hate lying to him.
But the floor was pretty slippery
after the janitor mopped it clean.
So my slip-and-fall story
isn't that far-fetched.

The whole ride
he studies me in the rearview mirror,
just like Sharon's been doing lately.

Georgia acts the opposite of her dad.
She barely looks at me.

I think she's mad
that I'm making her keep
one more secret.

CLUMSY

There's something different
about your craniofacial structure today, Dad says at home.

I slipped on the diving board at practice, I lie. Again.

Hmmm. Coach Baker didn't call me.

I told him not to.
Besides, would you even be able
to find your phone if he did call?

Of course. It's right here. Somewhere . . .
He starts sifting through a pile
of clothing and newspapers.

Dad, I'm going to bed.
My head's throbbing.

Wait! I've got just the remedy for that!

SOLVED

Dad flags down our waitress right away.
We need a bag of Pisum sativum *in a brumal state,*
and a large order of your spiciest number nine! Stat!

I translate the order:
a bag of frozen peas for my face,
chili fries for our stomachs.

The waitress gives us an odd look.
She delivers the peas quickly.

As soon as she's gone,
Dad slams his palm on the table.
Bud, this is serious.

I'm sure he's going to make me
fess up
about my
beatdown.

A team of mathematicians from South Africa
claim they solved the Riemann hypothesis!

My mouth forms a gaping
        zer0.

Dad leans forward,
gently presses the cold peas
to my swollen cheek.

Then he removes his glasses,
pinches the spot
between his eyes.

I worry
some fissure is forming,
ready to cleave and
        break
his brilliant brain,
like Humpty Dumpty falling
down
        down.

The waitress returns,
sets a platter of chili fries on the table,
then disappears.

How does that make you feel? I ask,
testing the temperature
of this news.

Dad looks up.
Hungry, of course!

We dig in,
taking turns
spearing wilting fries
with our forks.

Eventually he says,
*I feel equal parts
elated and
disappointed.*

I stare at the almost-empty
grease-stained basket.
We can always order more.

Oh, bud!
He nudges the last fry
onto my fork with a wink.
What I mean is
there are plenty more
mysteries to solve.

NEW SOLUTION

Dad may give up
the last chili fry,
but I realize he'll never
give up his dream
of solving the unsolvable.

So why should I?

Maybe there's a way
to crack the tangled equations
of my life
and find a new solution.

PAYBACK

I'm gonna pummel that fool into a pancake!
Liam declares, jabbing his fists in the air
when he sees my bruised face the next morning.

Don't even think about it, I say.
You can't.

News flash: Yes, I can.
Have you seen these puppies? Liam flexes scrawny muscles.

Liam! I shout.
Two more strikes, remember?
If you get sent to summer school,
I will be totally alone.
ALL. SUMMER.
If you want to help me,
stay out of trouble.
Okay?

He slaps a street sign,
elbows a hedge,
roundhouse kicks a lamppost.
Fine. I'll try, he huffs.

NO FUN PHONE

A few days after my little *slip-and-fall incident,*
Sharon buys Liam a cell phone.

He calls it a No Fun Phone
because it has
no games, videos, or data plan.

Just in case of an emergency, Sharon says,
handing it to Liam
but looking hard
at me.

Worst-Case Scenario #477:
RUNAWAY TRAIN

- If you need to jump from a moving train, wait for the train to slow as it bends around a curve.

- Stuff blankets, straw, or other padding into your clothes.

- Pick a landing spot before you jump.

- Get low to the floor, bending your knees.

- Jump perpendicular to the train, leaping as far from the tracks as possible.

- Tuck, cover, roll.

- BRACE FOR IMPACT!

GEORGIA VERSUS GRAVITY

At swim practice
Georgia takes the ladder
two rungs at a time.

I watch from below,
glad my own legs are anchored
securely on the pool deck.

She pauses, smiles down at me.
Want to know my favorite part about diving?

*Watching my tortured expression
as you climb that thing?* I reply, grimacing.

*No, Worst-Case Collin.
It's the moment
after my feet leave the board.
When it's just me
versus gravity.*

But, Gannet, I call up to her,
gravity always wins.

Exactly.
She reaches the top platform,
jumps up and down a few times,
which always makes my heart
flop around in my chest—
        anxious, helpless
like a goldfish
spilled from its bowl.

Gravity might always win,
but I've got a choice:
                    fall
                    or
                    dive.
And I choose to dive.
She bends her knees.
Preferably with style!
She leaps, twists, splashes.

When her face breaks the surface,
she spits an arc of water in my direction.

So can you, Collin.

T-MINUS 54

The day before spring break,
no one
        (not even the teachers)
can possibly pay attention.

Liam passes me a slip of paper
plotting a week's worth of epic adventures.
In the margins, I doodle
all relevant safety measures
in comic-book form,
adding some highly unlikely scenarios
with dramatic outcomes like
        stampeding rhinos,
        volcanic eruptions,
        and explosive diarrhea,
which crack Liam up, as intended.

In a singsong voice, Ms. Treehorn says,
Spring is the season for fresh starts!

Instead of grammar worksheets,
she asks us to clean out our desks
so the classroom will be in peak learning mode (oh, joy)
when we return from vacation.

Ms. Treehorn inspects my work space,
and calls it *Immaculate!*
Which is a vocabulary word
we haven't learned yet.
But I think it's a compliment,
because she smiles

so wide
all her teeth show,
        even the snaggly one on the far left side.

Then she glances out the window
at gray clouds, tumbling.

She promises extra recess
if we finish our tasks quickly,
before the storm hits.

RAIN

In the doorway
Georgia reaches

up.

Her palm opens,
           welcoming
                  each
                        wet
                            rare
                                raindrop.

∞ ∞ ∞

Of course Ms. Treehorn manages
to turn extra recess into
      a learning moment.

Bullhead City's annual average rainfall is only six inches.
This kind of precipitation is extremely unusual!

We're not in an orderly line
listening like we should be.
Our class has become
a noisy pack of desert coyotes,
yipping, nipping,
pawing the ground.
Waiting to be released
into the wild.

Ms. Treehorn sighs. *Go ahead!*

No one minds
getting soaked.

The air is warm and thick.
I'm grateful
for this unexpected shower.

I think the parched earth
is grateful, too.

We spin. We sing.
We stomp,
dashing water
from shallow, muddy puddles.

Tyson sings in the loudest
most obnoxious voice,
It's raining!
It's pouring!
The drugged-up driver
is snoring!

My body stills.
Something about those lyrics
feels too close for comfort.

Tyson sings louder,
Went to sleep,
crashed his jeep—

I cover my ears,
because this stupid song
dredges up

images
better left
submerged:
> Black rubber scars
> seared
> across gray asphalt.

> A metal guardrail, crumpled.
> A weak fence, clinging.
> A car
> > sinking.

Liam takes one look at me—
> at the red creeping up my neck and face—
and he understands.

Before I can say a word
or try to stop him,
Liam socks Tyson
square in the face.
Like a comic-book character,
his fist goes
> *ker-POW!*

Tyson reels,
> staggers,
> > > slips,
> falls
backward.
> His legs fly
> > UP!

His mud-splattered sneakers
have bright blue soles
I've never noticed before.

A bunch of kids gathers round.
Tyson whines and bellows,
covering his bloody nose.
At least he's not singing anymore.

I can't deny
that my skin prickles
with a fleeting spark
of satisfaction.
But this fades quickly
as reality sets in.

Ms. Treehorn rushes over
with one of the recess monitors.
I turn to Liam
before the teachers
escort him
to the principal's office.
We exchange
a small nod.
      Sometimes
      that's all
      friends like us
      need
      to say.

STRIKE TWO

Worst-Case Scenarios, Spring Break Edition:

Liam, grounded for breaking Tyson's nose.

Georgia, three hours away visiting her grandmother.

Collin, miserable at home with the Hoard.

What the heck am I going to do all week?

OCOTILLO

The following afternoon
I bike to the vacant lot
to clear my head
and devise a new plan.

I spot a clump of ocotillo
growing along the chain-link fence.

After the fluky rain,
swaying stalks
sprout oval leaves
and tufts of fiery flowers.

A hummingbird zips past,
                        pausing midair,
its so-fast wings
      blur-buzzing,
its thin beak
      nectar-sipping
      from red blossoms.

I watch until
it flies away,
wishing
I could do the same.

∞ ∞ ∞

When I get back home,
Liam is waiting

on my front steps,
his bike propped against the garage.

My heart feels like a grape
squished beneath a sneaker.
   Did I remember to lock the door?
   Did Liam go inside?
   Did he see the Hoard?

Dude! Where have you been?

Just riding my bike, I say, trying to be chill.
Aren't you grounded?

Not anymore! It's a Christmas miracle!

Liam, it's March.

Right. Whatever.
When I explained to my mom
that I punched that dirtbag
because he sang a song
about what happened to your mom,
she got these sad puppy eyes
and said she doesn't condone violence—
whatever that means—
but she understands why I did it.

Okay. I swallow hard,
trying not to think about that song,
wondering if Tyson really did sing it
to hurt me.

I'm still in trouble with Principal Rodriguez,
but Mom said you shouldn't be punished

for my stupidity. Liam snorts. *Which is a rude thing*
for a mother to say, in my opinion. But anyway,
you can stay over if you want.

Cool, I say with a shrug,
like it's no big deal.
I don't want to appear too desperate
even though I totally am.

Let's go! Liam says.

Umm. First I have to finish a few chores.

Chores? Really? He groans.

I promised my dad, I lie,
stalling,
to keep him
from coming inside.
As soon as I'm done,
I'll pack a bag
and come over.

Okay. You need help?

No, no. I shake my head.
Thanks, though.

Fine. But hurry!
He hops back on his bike.

I head into the house,
stuff my toothbrush and some clothes
into a duffel bag,

then close my bedroom door tightly
to keep the Hoard out.

Before leaving,
I write Dad a note
telling him where I'll be
for the next few days.
I tape it to the cupboard
so it won't get lost
among the disorganized heaps
of paper and utensils and dishes
covering the counters.

I pause on my way out,
wondering
if he'll miss me.

THE BEST WEEK

Liam and I have the best week.

We visit Miguel's to see who can eat the most churros (Liam).
We have a dance-off to decide who has the best moves (me).
We construct a contraption called a snot-rocket
to test whose boogers fly farther (it's a tie).

I help out around their house a little, too,
clearing the plates after dinner,
and offering to fold laundry with Sharon.
She pretends to take my temperature to see if
I've contracted some make-believe "laundrosis" virus.
But I know she appreciates my help.
And I enjoy her mom-ish company.

Plus, I actually like cleaning up,
which Liam thinks is ten times weirder
than building a snot-propulsion system
out of straws, rubber bands, and Popsicle sticks.
(This prompts Sharon to take *his* temperature, declaring that
he's most definitely suffering from
an incurable case of "brain-boogeritis.")

∞ ∞ ∞

Day by day
laughter   replaces worry.

Distracted by silliness, warmth, and
just being a kid,

I temporarily forget
about the Hoard.

Liam and I spend spring break watching cheesy movies,
inventing new games, plotting pranks.
When we swap Lindsay's hair conditioner
with mayonnaise and she freaks out,
Liam tells me I should add
Bad Hair Days to my orange disaster book.
  That's when I realize
    I haven't checked it once since I arrived.
     Which is surprising,
     and also
     surprisingly nice.

∞ ∞ ∞

On Friday afternoon
Dad picks me up.
He hugs me tight, which tells me
he did miss me.
I'm happy to see him, too,
but as soon as we pull into our driveway,
a familiar ache wracks my gut.
Even though I ate a lot of junk food this week
I don't think this feeling is indigestion.

My pulse quickens;
the tips of my toes tingle.

I pause on the front steps.
Do I have to go inside?

Welcome Home, the dingy doormat says.
I wish those words
were reassuring
or comforting or inviting.
But they're the opposite.

Dad looks at me strangely.
Go on inside, bud. He unlocks the door
and nudges me gently.

I take a deep breath
and prepare to face
my old foe.

∞ ∞ ∞

A week away
has given me
new eyes.

I knew our house was bad,
but it's funny
          (or maybe sad,
            or scary,
            or all of the above)
how a person gets
used to something
when they live with it
          every day.
The shock value fades
          over time
and you stop seeing
          what's real.

But the moment Dad opens that door,
the contrast between our home
and Liam's home
hits me like a sucker punch.

The smell is worse than I remember and
I see EVERY THING
more clearly than before, and
holy cow, I cannot believe
how many disgusting, nasty,
unnecessary, inexplicable things
are in my house.

I turn to my dad, to tell him,
We don't have to live like this,
but he's already shuffling
through the mess,
retreating to the basement.
Leaving me puzzled and alone
again.

REBOOT

On the upside,
spring break felt like
pressing the reset button
on a video-game console.

Sure, the Hoard thrived
in my absence.
Sure, my dad is acting
weirder than ever.
But I'm recharged,
powered up,
ready.

I will:
      solve this problem,
      clean this mess,
      and fight
            (if I have to).

∞ ∞ ∞

My orange book says
emergency situations should be
triaged
which means
to treat the worst first.

How can I triage
this house
when every room is
such a disaster?

I refuse to go back into
Dad's bathroom.

The basement is a lost cause.

I'm not feeling brave enough
to tackle the kitchen.

The living room isn't technically the worst,
but it would be nice
to have a place to sit again.
        I think the couch is still in there
        somewhere.

My work begins at dawn.

KA-BOOM!

It's Saturday
and Dad has to go
to the university.
Normally this would bum me out,
but I'm grateful for the chance
to clean while he's away.
He gets so jittery and irritable
whenever I try to tidy up.

I eat breakfast
(leftover muffins that Sharon baked)
then I get to work.

I sift, sort, chuck.
The Hoard didn't see this coming!
Ker-POW!
    Sha-ZAM!
        Ka-BOOM!

Three jumbo plastic bags swell
before I even reach the coffee table.

I carry them to the curb.
The garbage collectors will be surprised
to see so many bags outside
on trash day.

Hours tick by.
I'm on a roll.

The Hoard's hurting bad.
Which has me feeling good.

My stomach grumbles.
I'd eat that can of corn in the cupboard,
but the can opener is still missing.

It's okay. Lunch can wait
until the couch is excavated.

∞ ∞ ∞

Between flyers, pamphlets, coupons,
I find pages scrawled with numbers and symbols.

    Scribbles of brilliance, Mom would say.

I place them neatly in a folder,
in case they contain solutions
to the world's greatest mysteries.

Then, a slip of paper catches my eye.
    A checklist.

☐ Study for vocab quiz
☐ Make your bed
☐ Floss! (your teeth and the dance)
☐ Sprinkle kindness like confetti
☐ But, when necessary, fight evil
☐ Eat your veggies
☐ Say hi to Liam
☐ Keep your chin up ☺

I know Mom wrote this for me
a few years ago,
but I feel like

I was supposed to
find it now.

I tuck the list
into my T-shirt pocket,
pressing it close
to my heart.

∞ ∞ ∞

I work for a few more hours,
buoyed by the thought
of Mom's checklist
and excited to show Dad
the progress I've made.
I know he'll be twitchy at first,
until he sees
how much better
less mess
can be.

I hope he'll smile as wide
as Ms. Treehorn.
I hope he'll kiss
the top of my head and say,
Gee, bud,
what would I do
without you?

∞ ∞ ∞

It's nearly dark
when Dad finally comes home.

I hear him struggling,
breathing heavily.
            Cardiac arrest?
            Punctured lung?
            Fleeing a rabid raccoon?

I sprint to the kitchen
along a freshly cleared path.

My muscles tic,
ready for rescue.

∞ ∞ ∞

Thankfully
Dad is fine.

Well, not fine—
            madder than mad.
But not mortally wounded, at least.

His face is caught
in the doorframe,
sandwiched
between two giant bags of garbage
dragged back from the curb.

His whole body shakes.
I see panic
behind his glasses.

The door's been open
too long.

What were you thinking?
He yanks the bags.
He curses.

If you drop the garbage,
you can close the door, I say.

No! No! No!

Don't worry, Dad.
I kept the important stuff.
I was careful with your notes.
Drop the bags!

No matter
what I say,
he refuses
to let go.

SPLITTING

Black plastic snags
on the latch,
stretching
        until it splits.

Garbage spills
        everywhere.

All my hard work,
        wasted.

I can almost hear
the Hoard roar
with evil laughter.
Mocking me.
        Winning again.
                Beating me down.

The front door slams
        shut.

Dad stumbles inside.
His fingers
        tremble
as he touches rescued treasures—
old egg cartons, a cracked wooden spoon, knotted shoelaces—
checking to make sure they are
        okay.

But nothing about this is
        okay.

UNSOLVABLE

An hour later
Dad's still sitting
in the heap of garbage.

His eyes dart across
        each wrapper,
        each crumpled napkin,
        each expired coupon,
taking inventory of the precious things
I so foolishly mistook for trash.

I was just trying to help.
I'm sorry, I say.
Except I don't feel
sorry at all.
Just confused
and a little bit frightened.

I must be missing
some piece of this equation.

No matter how much
I stretch and pull and yank my brain
I cannot make
        garbage + junk + filth = happiness

I worry Dad may be
even more unsolvable
than the Riemann hypothesis.

HELP WANTED

The latch on the front door
broke when Dad crashed through
with all those bags last night.

Dad says
he'll fix it.
He says
he'll fix everything.

I'm tired of waiting.

I leave the house
as soon as the sun rises.

Miguel waves
as I ride my bike
past the taquería.
He hangs a sign in the window:
    Help Wanted

I have this weird urge
to stop, grab the sign,
slip it over my head, wear it
like a massive, awkward necklace.
Or leave it dangling
on our front door
for everyone to see.

Instead I pedal faster,
putting distance between
me and   the Hoard.

DRIFT

The shopping mall project
shut down indefinitely,
which means I can wander freely.

I take deep gulps of air,
            soak in the sun,
                    let myself
                        drift.
                            Usually
                            where my feet travel,
                            my mind follows

                    Today my thoughts chart
                    their own course.

            They tug me

                    back,
            back,
back
to memories
I usually keep
buried.

THE ACCIDENT

The bridge across the river
    narrow.
The guardrails
    weak.
The desert weather
    wet.
The other driver
    high.
Mom's hospital shift
    early.

The fog at dawn
    thick.
The current
    strong.
When it should have been
    dry.
The water level
    deep.
She couldn't afford to be
    late.

Bright yellow
double lines

did nothing
to stop

    the other car
        from speeding
            too far   too fast
          to avoid.

SINKING

It wasn't the crash
that caused the most
damage.

Neither
Laughlin nor Bullhead
sent help
fast enough
to that spot
in the river.

That invisible
line
between
here and   there.

Everyone called it
a fluke
but what if
someone had been
better prepared?

Maybe
she wouldn't
have been
trapped
inside that car

when water
replaced

air.

HUMMINGBIRD

After a good, long walk,
my mind feels clearer.

Sifting, sorting, confronting
memories of the accident
opened up new spaces.

I pause—watching as a hummingbird
hovers, darts, sips,
                              flies
                              free.

Ms. Treehorn told us
more than a dozen species
migrate through this area each year
in search of survival.

A new idea
buzzes around
in my head
until it's impossible
to ignore.

        If I can't defeat
        the Hoard

        maybe
        I can at least
                        escape.

Yes. That's it.
I'll become a hummingbird.

EMAIL

I bike to the library,
log on to one of the public computers
where I can send messages quickly
and collect replies
that don't take up space
on counters, tables, or sinks.

Organizing is simple:
> Just click, click, click.
> Then empty the trash can
> into cyberspace.
>> Without breaking a sweat.
>> Without breaking a door.
>> Without breaking a heart.

REACHING OUT

I message Georgia first,
surprised to see her online.

She says she's helping her grandmother
sort, scan, digitize
family photo albums.

Guess what?
No newborn pics of me.

Do U want 2 look 4 them? I reply.

NO, she types quickly.

Not the photos . . .

I know what you mean. Still no.

Actually . . .
I do. All the time.

I can help U look 4 them.
Someday. If U want.

I don't.

OK. If U ever change UR mind . . .

It's just . . .
What if . . .
They don't want me
to find them?

What if they R thinking the same about U?

Maybe @ 18, Georgia replies.

You'll buy a lottery ticket? Go 2 college?
Register 2 vote?
I send her a string of goofy emojis.

She sends a face with bulging eyeballs back.
I can look at my adoption files
when I turn 18.
Then you can help me
find them.

OK. Should I make a countdown calendar?

She sends a smiley face with the tongue sticking out.

I send her an alarm clock gif
and type the words,
T-minus 5.5 years.

Unlike Georgia,
I don't have
five and a half years.

I need to find someone
now.

SLUDGE

I return home
starving.
I scrounge around
for something to eat,
but our kitchen is
worse than ever.

In an effort to save
empty yogurt containers and
pickle jars last night,
Dad accidentally tipped over
a value-size vat of cooking oil
which has been leaking, seeping
through the junk mail and newspapers
that cover the countertops,
coating everything
with a greasy sludge.

At least the lack of
dining surfaces
gives Dad and me
a good excuse
to go out,
spend time
together
and pretend
life is normal
for a few hours.

CHECKMATE

We bump into
Tyson and his mom
at the diner.

Our parents make neighborly
small talk.
They're completely
oblivious
to their sons,
silently smoldering
inches apart.

The bruise under Tyson's left eye
is turning yellowish, a reminder
of Liam's pre-spring break punch.
I notice a second, darker,
fresher-looking bruise
on his chin. Who gave him that?

When he sees me looking, he sneers.

I lock my eyes
on the black-and-white
checkerboard floor.

You boys should get together this summer,
Tyson's mom says.
Tyson's been terribly lonely since Keith moved.
And his stepbrother can be a bit rowdy.
Isn't that right, honey?

Tyson grimaces, maybe because
        his mom called him honey

or his bruises hurt
or he can't stand the idea
of hanging out with me.

Whatever. I feel the same.

Perhaps the only torture
worse
than spending summer vacation with
the Hoard
would be a forced playdate
with my enemy.

The overhead speaker blares,
Farty, party of two!
Now seating the Farty party!

Oh! That's us! Dad says,
completely mortifying me
and rescuing me
all at once.

∞ ∞ ∞

He may have cracked a joke
when the waitress called our fake name,
but as soon as we sit down,
Dad grows quiet.

The first clue
that something is wrong:
            he orders a salad.

The second clue:
  when he thinks I'm not looking
  he fills his pockets
  with used napkins,
  crumpled straw wrappers,
  several packets of artificial sweetener.

He's hoarding, clinging to whatever
he can get his hands on,
trying to fill the unbearable
emptiness
that losing Mom
carved
into our lives.
And yet—
here I am.
  His own son.
  Sitting right across the table.

I want him to gather *me* up,
hold *me* close.
I want to talk to him
about so many things
but he's like the vacant lot:
  fenced off, shut down.

Maybe tomorrow he'll let me in.

10

I stop at the library
first thing in the morning
to check my email.

A reply from Aunt Lydia
appears in my inbox
with lots of XOXOs, exclamations points,
and, most importantly,
      a string of ten numbers.

T-MINUS 41

On Monday morning
the words
>Shopping mall

are written in red
across Ms. Treehorn's whiteboard.

Field trip? Liam asks.

Mr. Urvall, you just had an entire week off.
Welcome back to the world
of classroom learning moments.

Then more words appear:
>*Dead bodies*

Now Ms. Treehorn has everyone's attention.

It turns out
human remains were found
at the shopping mall site,
next to animal bones,
charred cloth, an ax,
and a broken ladle.

Funerary objects, Ms. Treehorn explains,
are the things we're buried with
when we pass on.

She tells us
her friend Charles
is one of the archaeologists
studying the site.

Along with the funerary objects,
his team discovered
a shallow basin
with a circular pit in the center,
filled with charcoal.

Charles believes
it's an ancient burial site
where cremations occurred.
Which means
the land is
sacred.

I could have told her
how special that land is,
and I'm not even
an archaeologist.

∞ ∞ ∞

Liam thinks cremation
should be the name of a new ice cream parlor.
All afternoon he won't shut up about
       banana splits with extra hot fudge,
       triple-scoop waffle-cone supremes,
       brownie batter blasts.
Until I explain to him that cremation actually means
       to burn a dead body.

Worst-Case Scenario #194:
HOUSE FIRE

- To minimize the risks of a house fire, install and test fire alarms throughout your home.

- Keep a fire extinguisher near cooking areas.

- Create and practice an escape plan with your family members.

- In the event of a fire, move as quickly as possible to the nearest exit.

- If there is smoke coming from under a door, or if a door is hot to the touch, do not open it!

- Seek an alternate route.

- If your clothes catch fire, stop, drop to the ground, and roll back and forth until the fire is out.

- Smoke inhalation can render you disoriented and unconscious.

- Cover your mouth and nose with a shirt or damp rag and crawl low to the floor.

- Contact your local fire department as soon as you are able to safely.

- Do not return to a burning building for material possessions.

- GET OUT AND STAY OUT!

SOS

Can I borrow your phone? I ask Liam after swim practice.

I told you, it doesn't do anything fun.

That's okay.
I just need to make a quick call.

What's the emergency?
Zombie attack?
Cyborg invasion?

Nope.

Prank call? Liam asks hopefully.

None of your beeswax, Matchstick.
I grab the phone
and walk over to an empty bench.

My hands tremble
as I dial the numbers.

The phone rings. Once, twice.

A gentle voice answers, *Hello?*

I can barely breathe,
let alone speak.

Hello? the voice says again.
Aunt Lydia
sounds so much
like Mom.

If I close my eyes,
I almost believe
it *is* Mom
on the line.

I miss you, I say, words spilling like water.
I really, really miss you.

Collin? Is that you?
Oh, I miss you, too.

I miss you a million times infinity
to the infinity power.

The voice laughs
and I remember
it's not Mom.

Your cousins and I cannot wait to see you!
It's been far too long.
Ogden's been making excuses for ages.

My dad? He has?

Gosh, yes! He always tells me
you're too busy.
When I got your email,
I was so happy, Collin.

So it'd be okay
if I come visit
for a little while this summer?

Absolutely!
We'll take you to the mountains, and the shore.
There's nothing like swimming
in the Atlantic Ocean.

I heard it's cold.

It's good for you.
A dip in that water
will put some hair on your chest!

I start reciting a chapter
about hypothermia to her
(which doesn't mention anything about premature hair growth).

Not that cold!
It's Maine,
not the North Pole.
She laughs her not-Mom laugh.
>   But hypothermia is no laughing matter.
>   Neither is puberty,
>   if Lindsay's pimply, hairy boyfriend,
>   AKA Catastrophe, is any indication.

WORRYING

While Aunt Lydia describes
all the fun we'll have,
the birds of worry
flap and circle overhead.
I try to shoo them away,
but they've come to roost.

She says:
beach, roller coasters, shaved ice.
     I hear:
     squall, whiplash, brain freeze.

She says:
hiking, camping, fishing.
     I hear:
     poison ivy, grizzly bears, hooks in eyeballs.

So, you'll come? Aunt Lydia asks.

This is my chance.
This is what I wanted.
But suddenly all I can say is,
I'll think about it.

WEIGHTLESS

I get to swim practice early
before anyone else.
I dive into the water
then rise to the surface.

I float on my back, weightless.

I close my eyes,
replaying the conversation with Aunt Lydia.

I picture a scale:
stinging jellyfish, riptide, squall, seagull poop,
biting ticks, poison ivy, burnt marshmallows,
capsized canoes, blisters, and slimy worms
on one side
                T
                      H
                          E
                              HOARD
                              on the other side.

DECISIONS

The scale tips.
I begin to sink.

I kick upward,
back to the surface,
take a breath.

I jet forward,
stretch my arms,
finding comfort
in the rhythm.

Pick a cherry,
put it in your basket.
One.

Pick a cherry,
put it in your basket.
Two.

After a dozen laps,
thinking and picking,
weighing my options,
I make a decision.

NO WARNING

Back at home
I rummage through the fridge
searching for last night's leftovers.
Then I head to my room
to finish homework
and read my favorite comic books.

An hour later the phone rings.
I almost miss the call
because the phone is wedged deeply between
the living-room couch cushions,
beneath several binders and files.

Hello? I say, thinking it's Dad
calling to check in.
He does that sometimes
when he works late.

Dude!

I recognize the voice immediately,
but I ask, *Who's this?* Just to mess with him.

*It's me. Your outrageously witty,
devastatingly good-looking,
ridiculously talented BFF.*

Oh, hey, Georgia.

Whaaaat? It's Liam, not Georgia! he barks.

I laugh. *Right, of course.
My mistake. What's up?*

I found your gym bag.
You forgot it after practice.

Oh, thanks.
Just bring it to school tomorrow, okay?

I'm one step ahead of you, Worst-Case.

I pause. *What do you mean?*

I caught a ride with Lindsay.
But she's going on a date with Catastrophe later,
so I can't stay long.

Stay long where? Liam? What?

I'll be there in a sec . . .
The line goes dead.

I run toward the front door
as the knob squeaks, turning.
I pray it's just Dad
home from work.

      It's not.

The latch is still broken.
The door swings
                   open
before I can get to it.

You left this at the poo—

EXPOSED

I'm fast,
but not fast enough
to keep Liam from seeing.

There are too many
obstacles,
      too much trash
      in my way.

Just when I thought
I'd figured out
how to escape,
      I'm trapped again.

I can't hide
our secret
any longer.

SHOCK

Shock makes people act strange.
It either gives you too many words
or too few.
      (Shame does the same.)

Liam stares.
His nose wrinkles.

I stare back, frozen.

Lindsay honks the car horn impatiently.

Liam mutters a single, *Whoa.*
He drops my gym bag onto the stoop
and gives me a super-weird thumbs-up.

I don't try to chase him
as he runs back
to the minivan,
speeding as fast and
                as far
                  from my disgusting life
                        as he can.

I don't blame him.

STUCK

My heart is a drum
banging out a frantic rhythm.
Tightly wound
worst-case scenarios
     unravel
         in my mind.

Once they gather momentum
       it's hard
       to stop them.
           A tsunami of what-ifs
           crashes with such force
           it knocks me off my feet.

What if . . .
    Liam never talks to me again?
    he tells Georgia what he saw?
    I lose my best friends?

       What if . . .
           everyone at school realizes Tyson was right?
           they crown him king?
           they banish me?

           What if . . .
               Sharon calls social services?
               they come to take me away?
               they put Dad in some sort of parent jail?

               What if . . .
                   the Hoard squeezes the breath out of me?
                   no one ever comes to rescue me?

CAN'T GO

I can't go
to school tomorrow,
or the next day
or any day
in this millennium.

I can't face Liam
or anyone
ever again.

But I really, really, really
can't spend another day
cooped up inside
with the Hoard.

FESS UP

To my surprise,
Liam is waiting for me
as soon as I step off the bus
the next morning,
his lips quirked
in a hard-to-decipher expression.
You. He points. *Fess up.*

I cringe.

Georgia joins us.
Yikes, Collin. You look awful, she says.

Good morning to you, too. I try to keep my voice steady
and my tone light, even though
I feel like I'm going to hurl.

Here, drink some water.
Georgia hands me a bottle from her backpack.
Everything okay? she asks.

I nod and take a sip of the water,
but I can't bring myself to speak.

Liam makes a face.
*Collin's been keeping
a dirty little secret.*

My entire body twists
into a gigantic tangle
of nauseous nerves.

Tell her what I saw yesterday.
He gives me a little elbow to the ribs.

I try to imagine how
the Hoard looked
through someone else's eyes.
My vision goes fuzzy.

Fine. If you won't tell her, I will.
Georgia, I opened the door to his house and . . .

I   feel   like   I'm   living   in   slow   motion.
I   am   SO   BUSTED.

This flipping genius
pranked his dad big time!

Hold up. What?

There were boxes and bags stacked
all the way to the ceiling.
He even detonated some stink bombs
to make the place really smelly.
Liam laughs, thumps me on the back.
It seems the student has surpassed the master.

Huh? I grunt.

I'm not taking credit or anything,
but I did train you
in the dark arts of prankery.
And what you accomplished yesterday

was an April Fools' joke
to rival them all!

It's not April first for another day, Georgia says, looking skeptical.

Exactly! That's the brilliant part about it!
The element of surprise was critical.
Right, dude?

It takes me   one   two   maybe three full minutes
to understand
what Liam thinks he saw.

Yeah, I say,
stuck between relief
and a totally bizarre sort of
disappointment.

Georgia crosses her arms.
Why didn't you mention this to us?
It's a weird prank, but we could have helped.

It was a spur of the moment thing, I mumble.

Georgia studies me,
scrunching her freckles.

You must've been working on that
for hours after you got home from practice.
Liam sighs. *Man, I would've paid money*
to see your dad's face last night!
I bet he used some seriously big words
to describe that mess.

I shrug awkwardly.

Can we come over today to check it out? Georgia asks.

Not today, I say, my voice still shaky.

Ugh. Why are you always such an excusenator? Liam stomps.
That should be your new nickname: the Excusenator.
It's like you don't want us around.

That's not true.

Georgia says, *You do have a lot of excuses lately.*

The thing is . . . I'm grounded.
Dad wasn't amused by my prank. At. All.

Oh, snap, Liam says. *Been there, done that.*
With great pranks come great risks.

Listen, I really do want to have you over,
I say earnestly.
Another day. Okay? I promise.

They agree but I feel awful.
Queasy, embarrassed, angry
that the Hoard is turning me
into a crummy friend,
forcing me to lie and   push away
the people I need
more than ever.

ESCAPE PLAN

Dad's not home
when I get off the bus
that afternoon.

It feels empty here.
Which is a weird thing to say
when I look at all the stuff
surrounding me.

My chest tightens; my teeth clench.
My hand reaches into my backpack.

I read one last chapter, and then
I chuck my orange book
          to the hungry
          Hoard

          like a zookeeper
          tossing a T-bone
          to a tiger.

From now on
I'll write my own
escape plan.

∞ ∞ ∞

I ride my bike to the library,
dash inside
ten minutes before it closes.

I log on to a computer
and send Aunt Lydia
a decisive email.

∞ ∞ ∞

When I get back home,
Dad's scribbling notes in one of his binders.
Hey, bud, he says without looking up.

I know I should
talk to him
about talking to
Aunt Lydia.

I sift and sort piles of words.
I can't seem to gather
the right ones.

Even if I did,
I wonder
if he would listen.

I'm starting to wonder
if he would care.

CONSTRUCTION

Late at night
when Dad is sound asleep,
I carefully, quietly
exhume and deep-clean
the guest bathroom
that's been blocked off for months.

The hallway leading to the bathroom
can be accessed from the back door,
which makes it easier
to sneak bags of garbage out,
unbeknownst to Dad.

Finally, I reclaim a small but important sliver of living space.

The whole ordeal takes hours
and it's seriously gross at times,
but I feel a sense of relief.

Finally, I can take a proper shower.

I construct a wall of cardboard boxes
with strategically draped sheets
which obstruct all views of the Hoard
from the guest bathroom and back door.
For a finishing touch,
I plug in some potent lavender-scented air fresheners
that I picked up at the Henny Penny
on my way home from the library.

Finally, I can invite Liam and Georgia over.

Finally, I can be a normal friend again.

T-MINUS 33

To celebrate the end of the swim season,
our team has a cannonball competition
off the highest diving platform.

Georgia wins for best form, of course.
Liam wins for biggest belly flop.
I win some bogus award for most cautious
ladder climbing.

The whole time
my mind keeps wandering
toward summer,
wondering
how it'll feel
to dive into cold, salty ocean waves
instead of pee-warmed chlorine.

And my mouth keeps twitching into a smile,
because I think I sort of understand
what Georgia meant
about gravity
and choices.

Falling
      versus
           diving.

DIVERSIONS

As soon as we towel off,
Liam says, *So, dudes, what now?*

No more swim practice means
more free time each afternoon.

This time I'm prepared.
I volunteer the tree in our backyard.
A project we can do together.

A diversion to keep my friends
from calling me an excusenator
and annoying me to death
until summer vacation.

They love the idea!

Georgia sketches out a design.
Liam says he'll bring
wood and tools from his garage,
which is great because
I've been stashing all the trash
from my cleanup in ours
and it's an utter disaster.

We'll stop at the Henny Penny
to pick up snacks and drinks
so no one will need to use the kitchen.

In a stroke of good luck,
I even found extra hard hats
lying around the vacant lot.

BUILDING

We work all afternoon,
     hammering,
     laughing,
     building.

After Liam and Georgia
go home for dinner,
I stay outside
to shore up a few rickety boards.

The tree isn't that tall,
but even a fall from ten feet up
could cause serious injury.

I'm putting away our tools
when I hear something
rustling in the branches
of a nearby tree
in the small community park
that our yard abuts.

It's probably just a bird
building a nest.

Harmless,
     I hope.

YARD SALE

We're having a yard sale this weekend, Georgia says.
My parents said you guys can bring stuff to sell.
It might be a good way to raise money
for more tree house supplies.

Can I sell my sister? Liam asks.

Uh, no. You cannot sell Lindsay.

You sure? Because she and her boyfriend
have been extra annoying lately.

Who? Catastrophe?

Yup. Although she calls him Stud Muffin. He gags.
Maybe I could sell him?

I'm ignoring you now.
Georgia turns to me.
How about you, Stud Muffin? She giggles.
I mean, Worst-Case Collin . . .

My cheeks flush.

Got anything?

If they only knew.

Yeah, actually.
Lots of leftover stuff
from that prank I pulled.

Great!

LOGISTICS

At home
stacks of cardboard boxes
and plastic bins
teeter toward
the ceiling.
  I pull one out,
  then another and
another,
  like a wooden plank
in the game of Jenga.

Wait—
how the heck
am I supposed to get
this stuff over to Georgia's house
before Dad gets home from work?

I check the clock.

I have one hour.

I need to move fast.

∞ ∞ ∞

The chain
  click
    click-clicks.
I shift gears,
pump my legs.

The wheels whir in the warm air.
A baseball card flutters
between rusty spokes.
  Fwap-a-wappa.
    Fwap-a-wappa.

Three more blocks to go.
  Click.
  Whirrrrr.
  Fwap-a-wappa.

Two more.
One.

Almost
there.

∞ ∞ ∞

How are you, babe? Sharon asks,
opening the door.

I need some help.

Her face goes yoga-calm,
despite the fact that
  dinner is burning,
  the smoke alarm is beeping,
  and Lindsay is screaming.

Tell me, babe.
I'm always here for you.

I've never seen her so zen.
It's sort of freaking me out.

Is your dad all right?
Is that Tyson boy bothering you again?

No, no. I wave my hand.
Georgia's having this yard sale
and I've got a bunch of boxes
to bring over to her house.
Except I can't carry them on my bike.
My dad's at work,
and I need to do this tonight.
Now, actually.

She takes a breath, nods,
like she was expecting me
to say something else
but she's relieved I didn't.
No problem at all.

∞ ∞ ∞

I carry the boxes
to the curb,
making sure
to close the front door
quickly
behind me.

Liam helps me lift everything
into the minivan.

Hang on, punks!
Lindsay pops her chewing gum
and hits the gas pedal.

Ten minutes later
we screech to a stop
in front of Georgia's house.

A broom rests in the crook of Mr. Wolcott's arm.

Georgia said you boys might be bringing a few things over.

Liam and I leap out of the car,
hauling the first load onto
the freshly swept stoop.

Holy moly!

This is just Collin's stuff, Liam says.

Interesting assortment, Mr. Wolcott replies,
which is a polite way to say
random junk.

VALUE

We spend Saturday morning
helping Georgia's parents
        set up tables,
        hang signs on telephone poles,
        stick price tags on trinkets.

I stare at each object,
wondering how to determine its value.

Georgia tells Liam
that no one will ever pay twenty bucks
for his stinky hockey pads.

Then some person
with severely malfunctioning nostrils
proves us wrong,
and Liam becomes
twenty times more obnoxious,
waving Mrs. Wolcott's brass candlesticks
over his head like trophies.

At three o'clock
the yard sale winds down.

Mrs. Wolcott packs up the unsold items.
In thick black ink she writes,
        Last chance! FREE!

We push the boxes to the curb.

If no one grabs these,
I'll drop them at the donation center tomorrow, she says.

How'd you kids fare? Mr. Wolcott asks.

Georgia's gray eyes
are wider than usual
as she counts our earnings.
Seventy-one dollars,
twenty-nine cents!

Twenty-nine cents?

Blame Collin.
He made his prices prime numbers.

Nicely done, Mr. Wolcott says.

Can we really keep it all? Georgia asks.

Absolutely. You earned it.

Let's get ice cream! Liam suggests.

But we need to buy more plywood for the tree house.

What tastes better, Georgia?
Strawberry swirl, caramel crunch, or wood-chip chunk?

I think we have enough for all of the above, I say.
I rattle off some quick calculations.

Well, I'm convinced, Georgia says. *And hungry.*

Liam cheers. *Cremation, here we come!*
Georgia and I just roll our eyes.

LAST CHANCE!

Maybe it's because
my belly is full of ice cream,
but back at home,
I barely fit
through the front door.

I angle my shoulders
just like the orange book described
in that chapter about breaking down a door.
I make my body a battering ram—SLAM!

Hey, bud!
You won't believe what I found
passing by Georgia's house, Dad hollers happily
when I tumble inside.
No one was home,
but her folks left these on the curb.
Can you believe it?
A spectacular deal
too good to pass up!

I stare past him.
One.
      Two.
            Three.
            Four.
            More?
            Cardboard boxes scream,
                    Last chance! FREE!

NOT A BIRD

My brain feels like a teakettle
left on the stove too long.
Steaming hot,
about to whistle,
           screech,
              explode!
I go outside
to cool off,
even though the temperature is
creeping toward the high eighties.

Tears sting my eyes.
I wipe them away
but more keep coming.

All I want to do
is smash something!

I pick up a hammer
and a box of nails.
I finish an entire wall panel
in record time,
channeling my energy
into the tree house construction.

With each *Ping!*
        Whack!
           Slam!
I feel calmer.

Until I hear that rustling
in the trees nearby again.

This time
I snap my head
quickly enough
to spot a streak of color
behind a clump of quaking leaves.
　　　Definitely not a bird.

There's more movement in the tree.
I recognize the bright blue
of Tyson's sneakers.
He's climbing down,
slinking away, darting
through the park
toward his own house
a few blocks east.

How long has he been spying on me?
　　　Was he watching the other night
　　　when I carried bag after bag
　　　from the house into the garage?
　　　　　Did he see me crying just now?
　　　　　Why can't he just leave me alone?

VOCABULARY

Reckless: acting with total disregard for safety, logic, or
    common sense;
AKA the way I'm feeling lately.
See also: a very cool-sounding nickname.

SEARCHING

The construction site at the vacant lot
may have shut down,
but the diggers and bulldozers
are still there,
locked up
like oversize mechanical creatures
at some freak show zoo.

I check to make sure
I'm alone—
      no protesters,
      no construction workers,
      no archaeologists named Charles.

If anyone asks,
I'm just a kid
with an interest
in local entomology.

I pull out an empty pickle jar
recovered from the Hoard
and unscrew the top,
punctured with holes.

My hands shake
as I tug on a pair of rubber gardening gloves.
I hope they're thick enough
to protect me.

I lift up rocks,
check nooks and crannies
until I find
what I'm looking for.

I have to be
        absolutely certain
I make
the right
choice.

Everything in my brain
says STOP!
        This is insanity.
        Do not actively seek danger.
        Abort mission! NOW!

But I'm learning that anger
is stronger than fear.

If Tyson thinks
he can keep messing with me
then I might just become
Tyson's very own
worst-case scenario.

SURPRISE

The next morning
Ms. Treehorn announces
a surprise desk check
to see if we've kept our work spaces organized.

Her timing could not be
worse.

My heart is not a dainty little hummingbird.
It's a woodpecker,
> *rap-a-tap-tapping!*
> > *Rap-a-tap-rap-a-tap-tapping!*
And my face looks weird.
I know this because Georgia says,
Collin, your face looks weird.

I am seriously second-guessing
my plan for revenge.

*Dude, you've got nothing
to worry about,* Liam says,
oblivious to what I've done.
Your desk is spotless.

Just as the *rap-a-tap-tapping*
slows,
> *rap-a-tap*
> > *tap,*

we hear
the scream.

When Tyson pulls his hand
out of his desk,
it looks like he's wearing a baseball mitt
made of flesh
        (which is as gross as it sounds).

CONVERSATIONS

I can't believe those scorpions stung Tyson!

> *He deserved it.*
>> *I didn't know he was allergic.*

> *No one did!*

> *How'd they get in his desk?*

Who knows?
>> *I can't believe he cried like a little baby in front of everyone.*

> *I'd cry, too, if my hand looked like that!*

>> *I can't believe Collin called an ambulance.*

I can't believe the EMTs stabbed him.

> *They didn't stab him. They saved him. That was an EpiPen.*

>> *An eponym?*
>>> *An EpiPen, you knucklehead!*

> *I've never seen anybody move so fast.*

Who? Ms. Treehorn? Or the EMTs?

> *No. Collin.*

SCORPIONS

They were just supposed to send
a message:

> Leave
>> my tree house,
>> my friends,
>> me
>>> alone.

I only meant
to scare him.

That's all.

TAKE BACK

I take back
all the times
I teased you
about that orange book, Georgia says.
Tyson's never been
very nice to us
but still . . .
I'm really glad
you knew
what to do.

∞ ∞ ∞

No one suspects it was me.
Instead, everyone's treating me
like a hero,
which makes me feel
like the most terrible
phoniest
fake.

T-MINUS 24

I revert to my old ways
and make up totally pathetic excuses
about why we can't finish
the tree house today.

The truth is
I need some space
to breathe
and think.

At the vacant lot
I wander and explore
and forget
to look up.

When I finally do,
the sky is plum-colored.

In the distance
a chorus of coyotes sings,
hungry for supper.

∞ ∞ ∞

I don't have lights
on my bike.

It's not safe
to ride
in the dark.

I should've left
sooner.

I pedal as fast as I can.
My muscles are jittery.

When I finally reach
a ribbon of familiar sidewalk
splashed with light,
I'm dripping with sweat.

A barking dog startles me.
At least it's not a coyote.

I veer left
and skid to a stop,
nearly wiping out.
A stocky boy
in ripped jeans
blocks my path.

Where're you going, freak?
It's Tyson's stepbrother, Jax.

Nowhere, I say, barely above a whisper.

You got that right.

Tyson appears next to Jax.
One hand bulges, bandaged.
The other tightens into a
mean knot.

Get lost, Jax.
Leave him to me, Tyson says.

Jax chuckles,
spits on the sidewalk.
Suit yourself, baby bro.

I grip the handlebars.
My feet find the pedals.

As soon as Jax turns to go,
and before Tyson moves any closer,
I jam my knees down,
pump my legs.

The chain clicks.
I burst away,
wheels spinning.

I make it half a block
at top speed
before my tires meet
a nasty patch of sand.

I'm careening
out of control.

Hurtling over handlebars,
landing on concrete.

I lay on the ground,
looking up at bright, bright lights
wondering if I'm dead.

I wiggle my toes,
check my vitals.

I'm alive.
　　　　For now.

I tuck my body
into a crescent,
protecting my head and stomach.

I'm an easy target,
waiting
for Tyson's blue sneakers
to appear.

∞ ∞ ∞

I brace for the first kick.
The first stinging
slap.

Nothing happens.

I look up.
Tyson's staring down at me.
The streetlamp is so bright overhead.
It's hard to read his face.

For a minute
I think he's wearing an expression
of pity. Or maybe even
worry.

Not possible. No way.

He's looking me up and down
like a bobcat stalking its prey.
That must be it.

Except his unbandaged hand is there,
open
        hanging
                in the air,
                    waiting.

He reaches out.
He pulls me to my feet.

We stand face-to-face.

I could have died from anaphylactic shock, he says.

Does he know I'm the one
who put the scorpions in his desk?
I steady myself. Fight or flight?
Which will it be?

I guess I owe you one, he says quietly,
looking down at his shoes.

Huh? I must've hit my head HARD.
Surely I'm hearing things . . .

*The doctor said I should thank you
for calling the paramedics so quickly,* he explains.

In the distance, Jax shouts for him to hurry up.

Gotta go.

Hey! I call after him.
Why were you spying on me
from that tree in the park?

He stops, rubs the back of his neck
with his good hand.
I *wasn't spying. That's my spot.*
I *climb up there to get away.*

From what? I ask.

Jax. My stepdad.
The fighting. All of it.

Before I can ask him more,
he disappears into the darkness.

Maybe I'm not the only one
with secrets
at home.

LOST AND FOUND

I fall into bed,
grateful to have made it back
mostly unscathed.

I wake up in the middle of the night.
I have to pee.
Can't wait until morning.

The house is so dark.
I'm so tired.
My muscles ache from my fall.
I'm not my usual careful self.

Halfway to the bathroom,
I find that can opener I've been looking for

with my bare foot.

It takes a few seconds
for the pain to set in.

I reach down,
grab my heel,
gushing warm, wet.

Even in the darkness,
I know
this isn't good.

I limp to the bathroom,
knock something over
with a crash.

Two bulbs flicker groggily.
I grip the edge of the sink,
slowly lift my foot,
pulsing with pain.

The gash is deep.
My blood, red.

My voice is a coyote's howl.
I want my mom!
I call for my dad.

I hear him clambering in my direction.
It's hard to navigate
the Hoard's dark maze.

What happened? He gasps.

I had to pee.

That's not how you pee, Collin!
Do you need an anatomy lesson?

No, Dad!
And I don't need some stupid lecture right now.

He stares at me.

DAD! I'm losing blood by the bucketful!

Enough with the hyperbole, Collin.

Enough with the vocabulary, Dad.
Please! Do something!

Okay, bud. Okay.
Let me take a closer look.

It's bad.
I think I need stitches.
Hurry.
Apply pressure to stop the bleeding.

He grabs a towel,
starts wrapping my foot.
I grit my teeth.

Let's get you to the emergency room, bud.
I'll carry you to the car.

I feel like I'm going to faint, Dad.
We should call an ambulance.

No, Collin!

Dad . . .

No one needs to come in here!

Dad, please.
That can opener is old.
It's rusty.
I might have tetanus.
Call an ambulance.

Calm down, he says.
You're fine.
Everything's fine.

Nothing's fine!
Get me out of this house.

He hoists me over his shoulder,
carries me
toward the front door.

My tears wet his pajamas.
My blood soaks through the towel.

6

Six is the number of stitches
zigzagging across my foot.

I lie and tell everyone
I accidentally stepped on a tool
near the tree house.

Georgia squints at me.
*You were walking around
a construction site barefoot?*

I nod, realizing what a lousy cover-up it is.

Doesn't your book advise against that sort of thing?
she prods.

Thankfully Liam interrupts, saying,
*I can't believe you actually came to school today.
Any smart kid would've milked an injury like that
for days.*

Georgia studies me a minute more.
She exhales, then reaches over
and pretends to tie
make-believe shoelaces
into a nice, tight double knot
over my bandages.

Thanks, I say.

She nods, picks up my crutches,
and helps me
get back on my feet.

T-MINUS 17

I hobble down the corridors at school.

Surprisingly
Tyson doesn't try to trip me once,
even though I'm the easiest prey ever.

The doctor said
my mangled foot
will take a few weeks
to heal.

But it's my heart
that hurts
more.

How long will that take?

∞ ∞ ∞

Georgia passes me a note in class.
She never does that.
I unfold it.
It says:
    T-minus 29

I look up and frown.
According to Liam's end-of-year calendar
there are only seventeen school days left.

When Ms. Treehorn turns her back,
Georgia makes a swimming motion.

Ohhh. She leaves for Camp Barracuda
in twenty-nine days.
Now I get it.

I smile at her
because I know she's excited and
it's a big deal to be chosen for the team.

Instead of smiling back,
she shrugs.

Then she looks me straight in the eyeballs
and mouths the words,
        I'll miss you.

Either that,
or she says,
        Kalamazoo.

Which is probably way more likely.
Yes, she definitely said
Kalamazoo.

LETTER TO MOM

I always thought
I'd miss you most
during hard times,
when I needed someone
to comfort me,
to help me
worry less, and
wonder more.

But that's not the case.

I miss you most
when good things happen, like
     spotting a shooting star,
       hearing our favorite song on the radio,
       watching someone special say the word *Kalamazoo*.

These moments
are the best
and also
the hardest
because I can't run home
and tell you all about them
and see how happy
they make you, too.

WAKE-UP CALL

I hold on
to a tiny seed
of weird, confusing
hope.

Maybe
this incident with my foot
will give Dad
a much-needed
wake-up call.

Nope. Scratch that.
Instead of acknowledging that
the Hoard is hurting me,
Dad continues feeding
the beast.

Now he's obsessed
with collecting medical supplies.

How do I tell him?

Not even a million Band-Aids
or miles of gauze and tape
could fix the fissure forming

between him
and reality.

Between
us.

LEFT BEHIND

I sit in the backyard
with my foot up,
watching my friends
work on our tree house,
my mind wandering, worrying.
>What would've happened if Dad *had* called
>>an ambulance?
>What if the paramedics or police *had* come
>>inside our house?
>What if they *had* seen the Hoard?
>Would that be a good thing, or a bad thing?
>Would Dad be in trouble? Would I?
>>That's when it hits me
>>like a patch of nasty sand
>>>that sends me flying
>>>over the handlebars again:
>>>>I'm less afraid
>>>>of being taken away.
>>>>>I'm more afraid of what
>>>>>might happen if

Dad is left behind
again.

MESSAGE

When Liam's not looking,
I borrow his No Fun Phone,
and hobble across the yard,
out of earshot. I dial but
Aunt Lydia doesn't pick up.
I'm actually relieved.

I know she would try
to change my mind,
to persuade me
to spend summer vacation with her
like we planned.
To be a normal kid
for just a few weeks.
        Carefree.

I leave a message
telling Aunt Lydia I have to stay
in Bullhead City this summer
with my dad.

EXCUSES

I call back a minute later,
leave another message.
I know she'll want an explanation.

Lies and excuses dribble out of my mouth:
 A really great summer job
   working at the Henny Penny;
 plus a spot at Camp Barracuda
   with mandatory summer practices;
 and a beautiful girlfriend
   named Georgia.

I really, really do not know
where that last lie came from.
Liam would be totally disgusted.

Georgia probably would be, too.

RATS

I think something bigger
than a mouse
ran across my bed
last night.

Even though my foot is bandaged
with layers of gauze and tape,
I could feel
its heavy warmth
scrambling.

Aside from being extremely creepy,
rats carry all kinds of diseases.

I may not be able
to leave Bullhead,
but I refuse
to sleep
inside
this
house
anymore
either.

Thank goodness
the tree house
is almost ready.

Until then
the car
will do.

T-MINUS 13

At least Liam
hasn't maxed out
his three strikes.

At least I won't be
totally alone
with truly nowhere
to go this summer
if I stay in Arizona.

FIELD DAY

In spite of the Hoard's filth,
I keep my injury clean.
I change my bandages meticulously,
apply the antibiotic cream
like the doctor instructed.

Thanks to this,
my foot heals
just in time
for Field Day,
when all the grades
play outside together—
       kickball,
       egg-and-spoon races,
       tug-of-war.

Instead of mystery meat,
the lunch ladies serve
hot dogs and hamburgers
and Popsicles
that turn our tongues
red, blue, orange.

There's even a dunk tank
       (which seems like a drowning hazard).
Principal Rodriguez sits bravely inside
wearing a shirt, tie, and swim trunks
       (which are not Wedgie Makers, thankfully).

The other teachers wear
weird clothes, too,
like jeans and T-shirts and sneakers.

Ms. Treehorn even brings
her fiancé,
some guy she calls
        Charlie.
He calls her
        Annie.

When they don't think we're looking,
I see their fingertips touch.

Turns out
he's actually
that archaeologist named Charles.

It's a little strange
to think about
Ms. Treehorn
having a life
outside
our classroom.

Sometimes I forget
that grown-ups
are just
regular
people.

∞ ∞ ∞

Ms. Treehorn takes me aside.
I want you to have this.
She presses the trilobite fossil into my palm.

Isn't this special to you?

Yes, but Charlie gave me a new stone.
Her eyes twinkle
like the shiny ring on her hand.

Her happiness is infectious,
and soon I feel like a balloon
filled with warm air.
Not so full that I'll pop,
but just full enough
that I spend the rest of the day
floating
next to puffy clouds,
      and maybe Mom,
      in the wide-open blue.

STRIKE THREE

Liam thought it would be funny
to fill some of the Field Day water balloons
with paint.

It was washable paint, but still,
it's no surprise
that Principal Rodriguez doesn't appreciate
Liam's sense of humor.

Especially now that he has to drive
a hot-pink-splattered
pickup truck
across town
to the nearest car wash.

∞ ∞ ∞

I think I'm more upset
about Liam's summer school verdict
than Principal Rodriguez
or Sharon
or even Liam.

TUG-OF-WAR

Aunt Lydia's messages flood my inbox.

She says she doesn't understand.

I want to tell her
                  neither do I.

I feel like that rope
we used for tug-of-war—   —pulled in opposite directions
        —fraying in the middle—

T-MINUS 6

I wonder if
taking something away
from the vacant lot
is causing all this
bad luck in my life.

I can't return the scorpions—
        they're living in a glass tank
        in the sixth-grade science lab.

But I do have the fossil Ms. Treehorn gave me,
        which also came from that same
        sacred place.

RETURN

To my surprise,
the fences are gone.

The ground looks like a blanket
spread out for picnicking,
infinite in every direction
until it meets the horizon,
where waves of heat
sew blue and brown together.

I lay the fossil down,
cover it
with a handful of warm sand.

Its home has changed dramatically,
but this is where
it belongs.

I wish I felt
the same.

T-MINUS 1

Today is the last day of school,
which means tonight is
our first official sleepover
in the tree house.

When I tell Dad
my friends are coming over,
he gets squirrely
until I assure him
we'll stay outside.

Before Liam and Georgia arrive,
I gather bug spray and flashlights.
I make sure the path from the backyard to the
guest bathroom is clear.
I stock a cooler with snacks and drinks.

Mom always made cocoa
when my friends slept over,
a cozy treat even though Bullhead is rarely chilly.
Dad asks if he should do the same.
      I'm shocked and touched
      that he remembers
      this small, nearly forgotten detail from Before.
But I can't imagine we have the ingredients
and I really don't want to serve anything
that comes out of our kitchen,
so I pass as politely as possible.

NIGHT SKY

The weather is perfect.
The sky clear.

A breeze dances,
      twists.

I'm doing my best
not to think about
what happens
after tomorrow.

∞ ∞ ∞

Georgia insists
we keep our
sleepy eyes
open
to watch
constellations
fill the dark spaces
between leaves.

There are so many ways
to connect
those spots of light.
So many shapes
and stories
up there,
depending on how
you draw the lines.

I see a cheeseburger! Liam says,
staring at the stars.

That's the Big Dipper, you dope! I laugh.

Hmm. Well, maybe I just smell a cheeseburger.

Actually . . . I smell it, too. Georgia sniffs the air.

Is your dad making us some late-night bites?
That would be awesome!

My dad? Doubtful.

The leaves rustle.
The breeze shifts.
I smell it now, too.

      Smoke.

          Coming from my house.

∞ ∞ ∞

I take the ladder
two rungs at a time.

Wow. Someone really wants a burger, Liam says.

My dad's not barbecuing! I yell.
I wince in pain

as my recently healed foot
hits the ground.

I race toward the house,
trying to figure out
what's going on.
The windows are all dark.
Dad must be sleeping.

The smell of smoke intensifies.
An alarm begins to wail
from somewhere inside.

Do you have your cell phone? I shout back to Liam.

Yeah, but it's just for emergencies, he hollers.

This is an emergency!

Oh! Who should I call?

*Georgia, help Liam figure out
the number for 911!*

I reach the front door,
uncertain and afraid
of what I might find
lurking behind.

SMOKE

I wrench and pull the doorknob.
The stupid latch is jammed.
I aim high, kick the hardware
with my good foot,
once, twice.

It won't budge.

I angle my shoulders and
heave my body forward.

I fall into pillows
of thick smoke.

Somewhere in the distance
I hear Georgia scream.
I hope she won't follow me inside.

∞ ∞ ∞

A box of powdered cocoa,
three ceramic mugs,
a blackened teakettle, forgotten.

Flames from the stove
leap, flicker, smolder,
moving greedily across the counter
where the cooking oil spilled weeks ago.

A gust of wind flings the front door open.

Emboldened, the flames begin
gobbling the curtains,
licking the walls,
devouring the papers,
        the trash,
                the so-called treasures.

I race to the sink,
fill the first container I can find.

I'm about to douse the flames,
when I remember
        water makes grease fires worse.

Dad! I shriek, my throat raw.

The smoke stings my eyes.

I frantically search for a fire extinguisher
but it's impossible
to find anything in this mess.
Desperate, I grab a wool sweater
from the pile of second-hand clothes
on the kitchen table
to smother the flames.

But garbage makes good fuel
and the fire grows
        too fast,
                too wild

for me and some lousy sweater
to extinguish
on our own.

I drop to my hands and knees,
move across the filthy floor
where the smoke isn't so thick.

I make it to Dad's bedroom.

The door's closed.
I press my hand to the wood
to make sure
there's no fire
hiding behind it.

I cover my mouth and nose
with my shirt
then stand and turn the handle.

∞ ∞ ∞

Dad's in bed,
deep asleep,
a pillow covering his ears.
I shake him awake.

He rolls over,
eyes wild.

Bud! What is it?
What's happening?

We have to get out of here! I shout,
between the alarm's piercing wail.

He sits up, disoriented,
disheveled.

I grab his hand,
pull him out of bed.

The cocoa! he shouts.
I was going to surprise you—oh! No!
I completely forgot about it!

We make it halfway down the hall
when something crackles and explodes.

The kitchen glows orange and angry.

There's no way
we can escape
through the front door now.

ALTERNATE ROUTE

I show Dad how to crawl
below the layer of smoke,
growing thicker each second.

A wall of garbage
blocks our path.
I hurl trash out of the way.

I pull him toward the back door
only to meet my barricade.
I think we can break down the barrier
together
if we move quickly.

Help me!
I can't do this alone!

But Dad's not with me anymore.

I scramble, coughing,
back down the hall.

Dad! Dad?

I see him
frantically ripping binders
from the shelves
in the living room.

What are you doing?
Leave them!

I can't! he cries.

Flames leap
into the room with a
frightening
            WHOOSH!

The couch becomes
a blazing fireball.

Dad! Stop!

He turns.
The back of his shirt
catches fire.

I tackle him,
dragging him to the ground,
using muscle memory
and super-strength
I didn't even know I had.

Stop! Drop! Roll!
I shout, tamping out the flames.

He pulls himself to his feet,
staggers toward the shelves again,
like a zombie, possessed.

I need these!
He clutches several binders
under each arm.

No, you don't!

The Hoard fizzles, bursts, flares
all around us.

Yes, Collin!
I do!
I need them!

I need YOU! I scream.
If we don't get out soon,
all this stuff
will become our funerary objects.
Don't you understand? I cry louder,
pleading with him.

Beams and floorboards
moan and creak
in distress.

Dad and I
can barely see each other
through the smoke.

Finally
I hear the thud
of binders
falling to the floor.

I feel his hand reach for mine.

Blue light
slashes through burned curtains.
A new siren wails.

Help is coming.

4

I cough and cough and cough,
but at least
I'm breathing.

I stagger
toward my friends.

We cling to each other,
counting:
        one, two, three.
        Dad makes four.

One. Two. Three.
Four.
My new favorite number.

COLORS

Orange
    pulse.

        Black sky.

Blue
    strobe.

        White stars.

Yellow
    tape.

        Black smoke.

Red
    trucks.

        White moon.

SWIRL

Fire engines, police cars,
      ambulances
            flood our street
                  with howling horns,
                        flashing lights, gushing hoses.
People in uniforms
      fuss over us.
            Others bravely try to tame
                a hungry, wild red-hot fire
                    on a dry, windy night.
I'm dazed,
      probably
            in shock,
                  my mouth empty
                      of words
                          and letters.
Instead
      I'm finding comfort
            in numbers
                for the first time
                    in my life.
Counting to four
      over and over
            and over again.
                One, two, three.
                  Liam, Georgia, me.
                    Dad makes four.
                    Dad makes four.
                    Dad makes four.
                    Dad makes four.

RELIEF

A crowd gathers.

Our neighbors
wear bathrobes, slippers,
        disbelief,
        fear.

And then,
seeing us
safe—
        relief.

I don't know
how much time
has passed.
        Seconds?
                Minutes?
                        Maybe even
                        hours?

I hold Dad's hand so hard
my nails leave my initial
                c

                        c

                                c

                                        c
                                        pressed
                                        four times
                                        into his palm.

EMBARRASSING

Dad stands in the middle
of the roaring, blinding night.

He keeps blinking his eyes.
Maybe because the smoke stings.

Or maybe because
when the walls and roof collapse,
our secret will be completely
exposed.

Or maybe he keeps blinking because
he's not wearing
his egg-shaped glasses.

       I realize he's also not wearing
       any pants.

He follows my eyes,
staring
       at our burning house,
staring
       at the crowd
staring
       at his bare chicken legs
       and his tighty-whitey underpants.

Oh, my, isn't this rather embarrassing?

We do the only thing
we can do:
       between our tears
       we laugh.

REVEAL

After a sleepless night
at the hospital
we return
the next day
to assess the damage.

The morning sun
shines down
on the gaping,
steaming
pit
that was
our home.

Yellow caution tape,
like ribbon on one of Liam's gag gifts,
wraps the perimeter.

The smell
is unlike anything
I've ever known,
singeing a memory
into my nose forever.

I think it's important
for Dad to be here,
even though I know
it will be hard.

To my surprise,
he isn't twitching.
Maybe it's the shock,
but he doesn't try to disappear

behind the tape,
to sift through
charred treasures.

He just keeps polishing
a new pair of eyeglasses
with the edge of his shirt,
like he can't believe
the image he's seeing.

He looks at the house.
He looks at me.
House. Me. House. Me.

Finally
our eyes meet,
sharing
the same thought.

His hand is tight
on my shoulder.

*Bud, what would I do
without you?*

THANKFUL

I'm thankful
we built the tree house.

I'm thankful
we camped outside.

I'm thankful
Georgia kept us awake.

I'm thankful
Liam smelled the smoke.

I'm thankful
I memorized those disaster preparedness chapters
that weren't so pointless after all.

Mostly
I'm thankful
Dad wasn't inside
when smoke
replaced air.

But

how can I be
thankful
for all those things,

and still be
thankful
for the fire?

AMENITIES

Even though Dad says
a motel is just
     a temporary living solution
part of me wishes
we could stay forever.

Each day, someone comes to clean our room.

The first time it happened
I thought there'd been a break-in.
Except instead of wrecking the place,
the mystery intruders
smoothed down the bedsheets,
vacuumed the burgundy shag carpet,
scrubbed the toilet.

And instead of stealing stuff,
they left us tiny bottles of shampoo and soap squares.

Also, the motel has these awesome things called *amenities*,
which include:
     a pool,
          where I swim each day;
     a vending machine,
          where I buy bags of chips and candy bars;
     a computer in the lobby,
          where Georgia and I send messages
          back and forth.

MESSAGES

It's easier to talk
with Georgia
from behind a screen
for now.

Some afternoons we chat
for what feels like ten seconds
but must really be a few hours,
because the clerk at the front desk
gets super cranky
and eventually yells,
Scram, boy!
Quit hoggin' the interweb!

GONE

Everything is
gone.

Well, technically
    unsalvageable.
    That's the word
    the insurance man uses.

Irreplaceable
is the word
my dad prefers.

    Good riddance
    are the words
    I choose
    but do not share,
    because
    Dad is
    fragile.

    At least he's not
    unsalvageable.

LOSS

I'm only sad
about the loss
of one thing:

    My favorite photograph of Mom

I tell this to only
one person:

    Georgia

THE HUMAN HEART

Georgia says
there is space inside
the human heart
for infinite love
and infinite sadness
and all the messiness
in between.

Is that one of your grandmother's proverbs? I ask.

Nope, she types.
*Found that nugget of wisdom
inside a fortune cookie.*
She sends a smiley-face emoji
followed by a single ♥

If the human heart
can (apparently) stretch to fit
an entire, infinite universe
of emotion,
why do I feel
as though mine
might burst?

PERENNIAL

Mom was wrong.
She said we had to buy
new flowers each year
because annuals die
and don't come back.

But a few days after the fire,
I find a yellow flower
poking its head
toward the sunshine.

Even though no one
has touched
our window boxes
in years.

Even though
everything else around it
is blackened with soot.

I wonder if this tiny
miracle
is like the ocotillo plant—
      quiet,
        protecting itself
until the rains
      (or fire hoses)
drench its roots
and wake it up.

CONFESSION

Liam opens the door
to his house.
I stare down at a crack
in the front steps,
trying to decide what to say.

I haven't seen my friends much since the fire.
Sharon begged us to stay at their house,
but Dad and I opted for the motel
until things get settled.

Today I finally feel ready for a visit.

Here. Liam hands me a cup of Jell-O and a spoon.
We sit on the steps,
poking the jiggly snack.
Why didn't you tell me
what was really happening, dude?

I just . . . couldn't.

I thought I was your best friend?
Your brother-from-another-mother?

You are.

I lift my eyes,
even though they feel
heavy as two dumbbells.

I'm trying to find a way
to explain something
that I still don't totally understand myself.

Remember that movie you made us watch?

He wiggles his spoon. *The Blob?*

No. The one about the creature from outer space.

What about it?

The main character really wanted to tell everyone
where he came from, but he couldn't.
Because he had to protect his home planet and his alien family
from being studied or attacked or worse.

I don't know if this makes any sense,
but right now it's easier to talk
          sort of sideways
about a movie,
than directly
about real life.

Liam finishes his Jell-O
in one giant, slurpy gulp.
He uses the back of the spoon
to scratch his head,
which usually means he's thinking.

My mom thought something was up.
She's been bugging me for months.
I told her to stop overreacting.
She's going to kill you, you know?

With her yoga-boa arms?

Yup. Watch out. He chuckles.
What's your special book say about that?

Well, the book's gone.
But I'm pretty sure
there are worse ways to go.

ONE CONDITION

I don't think you should call me
Matchstick anymore, Liam says.
It doesn't feel right, because, well, you know.

Fine. And you can stop calling me Worst-Case Collin.

Deal. With one condition, he says.

I'm afraid to ask . . .

It's nothing skullduggerous.

Is that even a word? I ask.

How should I know?
I'm the one going to summer school.
Did you know Tyson's going to be there, too?
Talk about torture.
Anyway, I'll stop calling you Worst-Case Collin,
if you agree to stop worrying so much.
I filled in the first few pages for you.
Maybe this will help.

Liam reaches into his pocket,
pulls out a small green notebook.

On the front
in his crooked handwriting, it says:
      Best-Case Collin's
      Best-Case Scenario Handbook.

BEST-CASE SCENARIO #1:
WINNING THE LOTTERY

---

* If you win the lottery,

* claim your prize.

* Then donate all the money to your best friend Liam.

* THANKS, DUDE!

BEST-CASE SCENARIO #2:
RIEMANN HYPOTHESIS

---

* If your dad solves the Riemann hypothesis and wins a million dollars,

* book some plane tickets to Disney World

* and bring your best friend Liam.

* GOOD TIMES!

BEST-CASE SCENARIO #3:
TACOS

---

* If Miguel accidentally adds an extra zero to your order and delivers sixty tacos instead of six,

* grab the hot sauce

* and call your best friend Liam.

* CHOW DOWN!

DEATH BY HUGGING

This is awesome.
I mean it.
Thanks, Liam.

You have to fill in the rest.

I will, I say.
I promise.

Out of nowhere,
he flings his arms around me.
I'm really going to miss you this summer, dude.

Uhhh, me, too.

Promise one more thing?

You're so demanding.

He squeezes me tighter.
Promise you won't have too much fun in Maine without me?

I'll try.
But Liam, I rasp, *I really can't breathe.*

Best-case scenario #47: Death by Hugging.

Wow. Who knew you were such a softie? I tease.

You think a softie would have killer pythons like these?
He releases me then flexes his chicken arms.

You've totally been doing yoga with your mom.

Sounds like someone's jealous of these guns.
Pow! Pow! Pow!

Admit it! I laugh.

Fine. I'm a multidimensional man-boy.
I do yoga!
No shame in that.
At least that's what Georgia says.
And you listen to everything she says, so . . .

My cheeks blaze.

He points a finger at me.
Ha! I knew it!
You like her, don't you!?
Your turn—admit it! Admit it!

I wind up to give him a good wallop,
but then he says, *I think she likes you, too.*

His words stop me mid-slug.

For literally the first time ever
I actually hope
that Liam's right.

WORRY

It's not like some overnight cure or anything,
but Liam's silly book helps.

It's good to be prepared,
but worry took up
a lot of space
in my heart
and my head.

I'm better off
without quite so much of it
cluttering me up.

TYSON

Dad's talking to
      an insurance guy,
      a police officer,
      some neighbors.

I'm standing on the sidewalk,
waiting.

It's getting hot out.
I want to escape
to the tree house
where it's shady,
but the caution tape says
it's off-limits.

Hey. Tyson's voice makes me jump.

Then I remember
the promise I made to Liam
about worrying less.
And I remember how it felt
to be brave
when I pulled Dad
away from the flames.

Hey, Tyson says again, inching closer to me.

What? I reply.

Bummer about the fire.
His words are slow and quiet,
not sharp and mean, like usual.

That really sucks.

I shove my hands in my pockets.

My dad walks toward the car, waves.
I have to go, I say.

Hey. I saw you . . .

I stop.

Carrying all those bags one night.
I heard you crying.

Just. Shut. Up. Please.

Geez. Chill out, Sweaty Betty.

No! Don't tell me what to do.
And stop calling me names!

Whoa. Someone grew a backbone.

I narrow my eyes to little slits.

He takes a step back.
Look, if I'd known
what was really going on,
that you were being suffocated in there
by all that crap, like everyone's saying,
maybe I wouldn't have acted
like such a jerkwad.

I start to walk away, but he stops me.

What I'm trying to say is . . .
I'm kinda . . . sorry. Okay?

I pause. I swallow hard.
And if I'd known
about your allergies,
I would never have put those
scorpions in your desk.

His head whips around. *Huh?*
I'm sure he's going to punch me.

His eyebrows arch.
He snorts, then shrugs.
Maybe we could call it even?

I blink, straighten my shoulders. *Maybe.*

Okay. He nods.

I'm not sure if this counts
as an official truce,
and it definitely doesn't feel
like friendship,
but at the very least
it's something better
than before,
and right now
that's enough.

∞ ∞ ∞

Nice to see you and Tyson chatting, Dad says
as we drive back to the motel.

That was the most we've said to each other in years, Dad.

Really? He looks surprised.

Really.

Guess I've missed a lot lately, he says, a little sadly.

Remember that diving board incident?
Secrets, like worries,
seem like silly things
to collect these days.

*Of course! I filed a complaint with the athletic department.
Demanded they increase the foot-friction-factor
of their equipment.*

You didn't. Please tell me you didn't.

I absolutely did! It was unsafe!

Our house was unsafe.

Even though it's true,
as soon as I say the words,
I regret them.

There's a rawness
to this particular truth
too tender
to touch
yet.

So I tell him the truth
about something else.
Tyson busted up my face, Dad.
That's what really happened.
I didn't slip. He's been picking on me
for a while. But we're okay now. I think.

He lets out a long breath.

I should've told you, I say.

I wish you had, bud.
I really, truly wish you had.

I know, but—

His expression shifts, lightens.
Because now your poor swim team
has an extremely sticky diving board to deal with.

I laugh and a smile creeps onto his face
for the first time
in days.

∞ ∞ ∞

We drive the next few miles in silence.
Dad's crinkled forehead tells me
there's a storm of thoughts
brewing and thundering in his mind.

I wish I could see inside.
I wish I could understand.
I wish I could help.

I've missed a lot lately, he repeats. *Too much.*
And I'm sorry for that.

He takes one hand off the steering wheel.
He finds my shoulder and gives it a squeeze.

I'll make it up to you, bud.

The last time he said that
he gave me a bag of junk.
Even though
things are improving,
I still don't really know
what to expect.

LITTLE BY LITTLE

Dad takes me to a mini-golf course
down the road from our motel.

We have such a good time
that we return to play
on Wednesday, Thursday, and Friday.

Spending this time together
is a million times infinity to the infinity power better
than any bag of junk.

At first
our conversations are like
our putts:
> short,
> a little wacky,
> frequently ricocheting backward.

For Dad,
mathematical theorems and proofs
are easier topics than
feelings.

At least we're talking.
It's a start.

DCS

It turns out
one of the people
Dad met with the other day
was from the Arizona Department of Child Safety,
       AKA the parent police.

When he tells me this,
I get panicky.

They're not going to take me
away from you, are they?

No, bud.
They just want us to attend some sessions, Dad says,
which sounds like a party invitation,
even though I'm pretty sure
it's the exact opposite.

We drive across the bridge
from Bullhead City to Laughlin,
along the same route
Mom used to take to work.

Out the window
I try to spot
that underwater borderline—

floating   suspended between   different places,

              just like me.

ROOM TO TALK

At first
the meetings with the DCS people are
    awkward
        like standing outside in your tighty-whities,
uncomfortable
        like itching powder down your pants,
    painful
        like finding a rusty can opener with
    your foot.

All I want to do is escape.
I can tell by Dad's constant fidgeting
that he feels the same.

∞ ∞ ∞

In the afternoon
I have a one-on-one meeting
with some guy named Mitchell.
He's got ridiculously bushy eyebrows,
a too-short tie,
and a lonely cactus in a really ugly pot on his windowsill.

I brace myself for more torture,
but thankfully he doesn't ask a million questions.
Actually he only asks one question:
Do you want a root beer?

I do.
He gives me a cold can.

Then he gives me lots of room
to talk if I want, or not.

After I finish my soda,
and read all the goofy comics
taped to the wall behind his desk—
        the kind that Mom would have found hysterical,
I decide maybe he's not so bad after all.

It'd probably be rude
not to say anything,
so I recite a passage from my
old orange book:
        the chapter about pythons.

The one that says it's practically impossible
to escape a squeezing snake on your own.
The one that says
        it's okay to need help sometimes.

I'm glad you feel that way, Mitchell says.
Underneath his eyebrows,
his eyes are actually pretty friendly-looking.
That's why we're here.

SWIMMING

Dad asks me to give him
swimming lessons
in the motel pool.
He says there are lots of things
he'd like to learn
to do better.

I start with sidestroke, my favorite.
Show him how to pick a cherry,
put it in the basket.
> *One.*

Pick a cherry,
put it in the basket.
> *Two.*

The cherries,
> like the memories we're making,
don't weigh us down.
> They do the opposite.

UNKNOWNS

Dad tells me he's been talking
to the counselors and doctors.
We all agree
that I should get some additional help.
I'm going to spend some time
at a hospital of sorts, Dad replies.

Why? I say, startled. *The burn on your back is healing well.*
The doctors said you have no serious injuries.

That's mostly true, bud.
Except I need to work on other parts of myself.
So that I can keep you safe.

What do you mean?

There are special therapies and support groups
for people struggling with compulsive hoarding disorder.
I'll be gone a few weeks, and then we'll see.
These sorts of things don't heal overnight.

But everything's getting better. You seem better!

I know. However, it's a bit like my equations—
some solutions are more complex than others.

Because there are so many unknowns?

Exactly, bud.
Thankfully that's never stopped me from trying.
Why should this be any different?

STARTING OVER

I'm fighting the urge to worry.
> Afraid things could go back to the way they were.
> Afraid things will change too much.

What will happen to me while you're gone?
I can't stay here by myself.

Of course you can't. Dad kneels down.
I think you should visit Aunt Lydia..
She tells me you made all sorts of plans together.

She told you?
Are you mad?

Not at all.
I'm proud of you.
For being brave.
For seeing things
I couldn't see, didn't want to see.
Things that are still hard for me
and probably always will be.
Things that will take time.

He takes a breath, pulls me close.
Which is why you should go
spend a few weeks in Maine this summer.

I'll miss you, I say, fighting back tears.

You'd better! He laughs.

You're really not mad
I reached out to Aunt Lydia?

Mad? No. Maybe a little jealous, though.
Hiking, camping, fishing?
Sounds like fun to me.

Aunt Lydia promised beaches and roller coasters, too, I say,
surprised but pleased that these activities
no longer feel worthy of so much fear.

Aww, way to rub it in! He musses my hair.
When you come back in July,
I'll try harder. I'll get the help I need.
We'll start over, take things day by day.
We'll move to a new house.
A clean house.

With a backyard?

Sure.

With enough space for a tree house,
and a superdeluxe mini-putt course?

I'll see what I can do, he says.

It sounds almost too good
to be true,
like sinking a hole in one.
        And maybe it is.
        But maybe it's not.

I wrap my arms
around his barrel chest.

Even in this crazy heat,
he's wearing a wool sweater vest.
It smells like barbecued sheep.
It scratches my cheek.
And yet, it's one of the things
I love about him.

What do you think, bud? Deal?

Spectacular deal, I say.
Too good to pass up.

JAWS

A few days later,
a demolition crew arrives
at our old house.

The wrecking machine
has the jaws
of a T. rex.

I watch
as it chomps down
on charred wood.

Its steel teeth
peel back singed boards
like skin,

exposing blackened guts
that were once
the Hoard.

BLOSSOM

What do we have here? Mitchell asks
when Dad and I stop by the DCS offices
in the afternoon.

I hand him a terracotta pot
filled with wet dirt,
fresh green leaves,
and a small yellow blossom.

A survivor, I say.
*The demo crew helped me
rescue it from our window box
before they tore down the house.*

Mitchell gives me a wide, grateful smile.
His eyebrows squash together, forming one
very impressive unibrow.

Dad nods in approval
and pulls the blinds open,
letting sunshine pour in.
Much better.

Mitchell places the pot
on the windowsill next to his cactus
        (which is still ugly,
                but at least it's a little less
                lonely-looking now).

SMILE

Before Georgia leaves
for Camp Barracuda
and I leave for Maine,
she comes to say goodbye
in person.
> Which means I can't hide
> behind a computer screen anymore.

I have something for you, she says.

She places a small pocket mirror
in my palm.

*I can't replace
your favorite photograph,
but this should help.
In case you need to remember
your mom's smile.*

Then she gives me
one more thing:

> A kiss!

KISS

I'm dying.
    Kaput.
    Gonzo.
    Adios, amigos.

I will see my mother's smile again (in heaven)
just like Georgia promised
before she planted

    that kiss!

Which stopped my heart from beating

    completely.

And killed me

    dead.

NOT DEAD

Turns out
I'm still alive.

Not dead.

Just suffering
from severe shock.

And maybe

      LOVE.

Which feels
      just as terrifying
      and horrifying
      and exciting
      as every worst-case scenario I ever studied.

Except *this*
      I am totally, utterly unprepared for.

And maybe that's what makes it
      so great.

KALAMAZOO

Mrs. Wolcott honks the car horn.
Georgia turns to wave
one last time.

My lips form the word *Kalamazoo.*

I see Georgia
through the passenger window.

Kalamazoo, too! she mouths.

My cheek is still
burning
as the car drives
away.

I unwrap my fingers
and hold the mirror
up.

It catches the sunlight
and then

I see
Mom's smile
smiling back at me.

Just like Georgia promised.

ACKNOWLEDGMENTS

I didn't have a bright orange book of instructions to help me write and revise this story, but fortunately many excellent people guided me through the process. Many thanks to Christa Heschke, Daniele Hunter, and McIntosh & Otis for championing my work and emboldening me to take creative risks. Thanks to my amazing editor, Julie Bliven, for seeing the potential in Collin's story and for loving these characters as much as I do. Your wisdom, patience, and keen editorial eye are unparalleled. To the wonderful team at Charlesbridge, including Kristen Nobles, Donna Spurlock, Jordan Standridge, and copyeditor Hannah Mahoney. I am so grateful for your skill, dedication, and hard work.

My critique partners and writing pals saved me from disaster on multiple occasions. Special thanks to Erin Cashman, Diana Renn, Sandra Waugh, Kip Wilson, Linda Elovitz Marshall, Suzanne Warr, Craig Bouchard, and everyone in my Littleton and Concord kidlit writing groups. Shout-outs to the Lucky 13s, the Electric Eighteens, and the wonderful folks at the Writers' Loft, and The Room to Write.

Kwame Alexander's New England SCBWI keynote speech inspired me to give verse a shot. Sarah Tregay maintains one of the most comprehensive lists of novels-in-verse on the internet; thank you for introducing me to the brilliance of Karen Hesse, Nikki Grimes, Thanhha Lai, K.A. Holt, Sarah Crossan, Helen Frost, Margarita Engle, Sharon Creech, Caroline Starr Rose, Elizabeth Acevedo, and many more. Their books became refuges, treasured teachers, and poetic playgrounds. I was lucky to learn from some of the best, including Emma D. Dryden, Sonya Sones, Andrea Davis Pinkney, Ellen Hopkins, and Padma Venkatraman. Your encouragement was a life raft.

Utmost appreciation to all the librarians, teachers, and booksellers who help put books in the hands of young readers. Hometown hugs for my local independent bookstore, the Silver Unicorn in Acton, Massachusetts. High fives to my magnificent

Middle Grade Book Clubbers. Keep reading and writing. I can't wait to read *your* books one day!

I consulted many sources while researching this story, including the work of Tracy Schroeder, Jessie Sholl, and Kimberly Rae Miller, as well as the work of the following doctors: David F. Tolin, Gail Steketee, Randy O. Frost, Michael A. Tompkins, Suzanne A. Chabaud, Tamara L. Hartl, Fugen Neziroglu, and Katherine Donnelly. Additional information was provided by the American Psychiatric Association, the National Alliance on Mental Illness, the International OCD Foundation, National Institute of Mental Health, and the World Health Organization.

My family and friends fill my life to the brim with love. Thank you all, for everything and every thing. My fascination with words, my insatiable curiosity about the world, and my love of storytelling are gifts from my mother—a poet and so much more. My father is a lighthouse, guiding me to shore time and time again. When my debut novel released, my in-laws practically converted a hair salon in Ontario, Canada, into a bookstore, proudly displaying my book alongside shampoos and conditioners, handselling dozens of copies to well-coiffed readers. I am grateful to be part of your *famiglia*.

Whenever a task feels daunting (like writing an entire book), my father reminds me to do one thing at a time. That's exactly how I wrote this story—word by word, line by line, page by page. And believe me, it was slow going, especially with two small kiddos at home. In fact, the majority of this book was written in my car, parked outside my local grocery store while my daughters napped in their car seats. (It's not an official title, but I do consider myself the Writer-in-Residence of the Market Basket parking lot. Ah, the writing life is glamorous indeed.) AJ & FJ, despite your challenging sleeping habits, you are the most wonderful children. I love you infinity times infinity. And of course, Stefano. You are my Best-Case Scenario.

According to recent studies, compulsive hoarding disorder affects between 2 percent and 6 percent of the population, and is characterized by excessive accumulation of and difficulty discarding possessions, regardless of their value. Some researchers believe the actual numbers are higher, as hoarding often remains unreported, unrecognized, and untreated. In America alone, approximately six to nineteen million people cope with severe hoarding tendencies. Many of those impacted are children like Collin, who must learn to navigate daily risks of physical and psychological harm.

If you or someone you know is struggling with the effects of hoarding, there are organizations available to help. You can find resources, support groups, and access to trained health professionals through Children of Hoarders (www.childrenofhoarders.com), Minor and Youth Children of Hoarding Parents (www.mycohp.com), and the National Alliance on Mental Illness (www.nami.org; NAMI HelpLine: 800-950-6264).

Stories have incredible power, and I hope this one will help build empathy, raise awareness, and reduce the stigma around hoarding. In 2018 the World Health Organization finally classified hoarding disorder as a medical condition, which is starting to spur much-needed research, education, outreach, and intervention for the benefit of children growing up in hoarding households.